Anna's Heart

Wilderness Brides, Book 2

By Peggy L Henderson

Copyright © 2016 by Peggy Henderson
All rights reserved
ISBN: **978-1539357704**

Anna's Heart

Chapter One

"He's back."

The door screeched on its hinges as Patrick Hudson stormed into the cabin. Several pheasants, tied by their legs on a strip of rawhide, were slung over his shoulder. The boy dropped them on the table in the center of the room with a thud. He glanced around, clearly looking to see if someone had heard his loud announcement.

Anna Porter straightened and swiped the back of her hand across her damp forehead. She faced the boy. Her eyes narrowed, glaring at Patrick. When his gaze met hers, he stopped in his tracks. The smile on his face turned into an open-mouthed gape. He looked from her to the dirty rag in her hand, his eyes filling with growing trepidation. Water dripped from the rag onto the wooden floor.

Patrick gulped visibly. He shot a quick glance over his shoulder at the floorboards, then offered a tentative smile. His youthful eyes turned apologetic at the same time that they showed fear of reprimand.

Anna dropped the rag into the bucket at her feet. The brown water sloshed over the sides, leaving small puddles on the already-wet floor. She expelled air from her lungs through her mouth and her shoulders slumped, glancing

1

from Patrick to the floor to the muddy footprints the boy had left behind.

"I'm so sorry," Patrick stammered. "I didn't know you were washing floors. I thought Caroline was here. I wanted to tell her Trevor just returned, and he brought news of visitors that'll be arriving soon." He spoke fast, his words slurring together in his haste to expel his apology.

Anna held one hand to her hip while pushing the kerchief that covered her hair further back on her head. She stretched her sore back.

"Visitors?" Her forehead scrunched. "Lucas Walker left a few days ago, and now there will be more visitors?"

"Yes'm." Patrick nodded enthusiastically. Like almost everyone else, spring fever had clearly gripped the boy.

The unexpected visit from one of the closest neighbors to Harley's Hole had been a sure sign that spring was here to stay in these remote mountains. Snow still covered the tall peaks of the Teton Mountains to the east, but the meadows in the valley were already green and starting to burst with a multitude of colors as wildflowers emerged among the grasses. Although it was already May, spring came later in these mountains than Anna was accustomed to in Ohio.

"Sometimes we get snow well into June," Harley Buchanan, the old trapper for whom this small valley had been christened, had told her one morning several weeks ago when she'd let slip that she was longing for some warmer weather after the long winter months.

Anna sighed. She shot another glance at the mud on her clean floor.

"Caroline is down by the creek with Cora, doing laundry." Her lips softened in a faint smile. She couldn't be mad at the boy for tracking dirt into the cabin, even though now she had to start all over with scrubbing the affected floorboards.

She shrugged. What good was it to try and maintain cleanliness inside this cabin? Her efforts to keep some semblance of order and neatness in this wilderness seemed futile. The men who lived here had no appreciation for a tidy home and were as wild as their surroundings. Old Harley was the only man who respected her attempts. He'd scold the three brothers he considered his sons whenever they walked in with muddy boots, which had been quite frequently lately with the spring thaw and rains.

At least she didn't have to live in the same dwelling as the men. The cabin she shared with Caroline and Josie Hudson was kept neat and clean to her liking, and the men weren't allowed to set foot through the door. In order to keep her hands and mind busy over the long months of winter and spring, keeping the men's cabin orderly had become her personal crusade. Not that any of them who occupied it showed even the slightest amount of gratitude, aside from Harley.

"I can clean up, Anna."

Anna raised her eyes to Patrick's contrite voice. She shook her head. How could she be angry with the boy, who showed more remorse than three grown men would have done?

"It's all right, Patrick. I know the ground is muddy outside after the rains. Next time, remember not to barge in, and at least take your boots off first."

"Yes'm." The boy hung his head, then raised his chin to look at her with a smile. "I can fetch more water."

"That would be nice. There's another bucket just outside the door. I could use some clean rinse water." She eyed the pail at her feet. The water was so brown and dirty, the cloth she'd used for scrubbing the floor had all but disappeared from view.

Patrick nodded, then headed for the door. Anna stared after him. She gave a quick laugh with a shake of her head, then reached into the bucket to fish out the rag. She wrung the excess water from it, then dropped it to the ground and used her old broom handle to push the rag around the floor.

"I might as well wait for Patrick to return from the creek." Anna brushed some hair that had come loose from her braid out of her face, tucking it under the kerchief. She glanced around the simple cabin.

The main room served as both the dining area and the kitchen. The stone hearth and fireplace used up much of the wall opposite the door, and Harley's bunk, piled high with various animal furs, stood against the wall to the right. Anna's lips twitched in a slight smile. The old trapper preferred beaver pelts and buffalo hides to wool blankets.

The rest of the beds in the cabin weren't any different. Two small rooms had been added on six months ago before winter had settled into the valley, in order to accommodate the three other men who inhabited this cabin.

The twins, Travis and Trevor Wilder, were only eighteen years old. They might be fully-grown men in stature, but they certainly acted no better than adolescent boys most of the time. They were certainly nothing like their older brother, Ethan. Anna's eyes drifted to the other room, partitioned off by a curtain she and Caroline had sewn months ago using old pieces of cloth to give the area some privacy.

While she kept the main part of the cabin clean, and even Travis' and Trevor's sleeping area, Anna dared not move past that curtain that led to Ethan's personal space. She'd made the mistake of crossing past that curtain only once with the intent to air out the bunk and perhaps collect some laundry. Ethan had walked into the cabin at that moment, glared at her with a dark scowl his brothers always teased him about, and had told her in no uncertain

4

terms to mind her own business and to stay away from his belongings.

As wild as the Wilder men could be, none of them were as intimidating as the oldest of the four brothers. Nathaniel, the second-oldest and husband to her best friend, had been likeable from the moment she'd met him. Even the twins could be forgiven for their uncivilized antics, but Ethan Wilder was simply callous and rude.

Anna had stammered a quick apology that day and left the cabin in a hurry, Ethan's stare following her all the way to the smaller cabin she shared with Caroline and Josie. Anger had overtaken the embarrassment she'd felt at the time. Ethan Wilder was an oaf, reacting with anger or a sullen demeanor rather than holding a civil conversation.

Anna had avoided him even more since that unpleasant encounter. During the long winter months, she'd tried to make the best of her situation. She didn't want to be here in this remote valley, so far removed from civilized society, and as soon as the weather turned warm enough, she'd finally bring up the subject of leaving.

As painful as it was to think about leaving her friend, Cora Hudson Wilder, and the other girls she'd considered her sisters, there was nothing for her in the wilderness. This was not a life she wanted, and more often than not over the last six months, she'd felt more like an outsider than part of a family. The other Hudson sisters had adapted well to living in the valley and got along with the Wilder men, but something was amiss as far as Anna was concerned. Even quiet and shy Josie had taken well to life in the woods, dressing in britches and going off hunting with Harley. Why had it been so difficult to make a home here?

Last spring, Anna had been full of hope at a new life in Oregon. It seemed like a lifetime ago. When Cora had told her she was planning to sell her farm in Ohio and move her three sisters and little brother to Oregon, Anna had gladly joined them.

The idea of traveling cross-country by wagon into the unknown had seemed worrisome at the time, but it hadn't been as terrifying as staying in Ohio with no family. She'd gladly left her painful memories and shattered dreams behind. Making a brand new start in Oregon had seemed like the right thing to do.

Things hadn't quite worked out the way they'd all planned, and the journey along the Oregon Trail had proven far from easy. When Cora had met Nathaniel Wilder, she'd had no choice but to put her trust in him to get them out of danger. There had been no other recourse for Anna but to go along, with the understanding that they would continue on their journey to Oregon come spring.

When Cora and Nathaniel had announced that they had gotten married, Anna couldn't have been happier for her friend. Cora had suffered enough loss and hardship of her own, and deserved a good man. Nathaniel adored her. That had been obvious even from their tumultuous first encounter.

Now that spring had fully arrived, it might be time to approach Cora and Nathaniel about taking her to Fort Hall, just as Nathaniel had promised to do when he'd brought them to Harley's Hole. He'd said he'd take her all the way to Oregon, but perhaps he could find her passage with someone on a wagon train heading west. All she needed was for him to get her to the trading outpost.

"Best to bring it up later today," she muttered. There was no reason to delay her decision any longer. If Nathaniel was agreeable to take her, she'd make preparations to leave, and they could be at Fort Hall within a month. That might be around the time the first wagon trains heading west would arrive.

Anna bent and reached for the dirty rag on the ground. She dipped it in the equally dirty water, and wrung it out. She'd wiped up most of the mud Patrick had brought into the cabin, but another good scrubbing with some clean water wouldn't hurt. She hung the rag on her pole which she then propped against the wall, and eyed the pheasants. When Patrick returned from the creek, he could de-feather the birds and she'd start on supper.

Anna grabbed hold of the rope and lifted the bucket. Brown brew sloshed out the sides. She opened the cabin door and took a step outside, squinting into the bright sunlight that entered the room. Her arms trembled from the effort of holding up the heavy bucket and, taking hold of the bottom with one hand, she swung her arms back and tossed the dirty contents as far as possible into the yard. A stream of loud curse words followed instantly.

"What in the blazes has gotten into you, woman?" a man roared.

Anna's heart sank to the pit of her stomach. She stumbled backward. A dark, imposing outline followed. Anna dropped the bucket and her hand flew to her mouth.

"Oh my goodness, I'm so sorry," she stammered. Her eyes widened, staring up at Ethan Wilder. He swiped a hand across his wet face while glaring at her. He looked ready to murder someone. Muddy water dripped from his face to the ground. His shirt and britches were soaked.

"What the hell do you think you're doing?" He advanced on her some more, his tone more furious than a second ago.

"I . . . I didn't see you." Anna clutched at the high collar of her dress in case Ethan reached out to strangle her.

"Can't you pay better attention to what you're doing, woman? I ain't that small not to be seen walking up to the door."

7

He did have a point. Ethan Wilder wasn't a small man. He wasn't overly large, either, but at this moment, he may as well have been a giant, the way he towered over her in his rage. His dark scowl increased as the seconds ticked by.

"Next time, look before you do something as witless as tossing a bucket of water at a man," he growled. The cords along his neck were strung tighter than a drum.

Anna's spine stiffened. Her mouth pulled in a thin line and she squared her shoulders.

"I told you I was sorry, Mr. Wilder," she said in a firm voice, emphasizing the mister. "It was an honest mistake, and I truly apologize for tossing the water out the door at the exact moment you decided to waltz into the cabin." Her voice rose with each word. She'd just about had it with his rude behavior. It wasn't as if she'd thrown the water at him on purpose, but he sure deserved it.

"Can't you ever say anything nice rather than throwing insults at a person?" she continued. "I'd be more than happy to wash your soiled clothes to make amends for what I did. I doubt you would have apologized for tracking mud into the cabin that I just spent hours cleaning." To make her point, she directed her eyes to his dirty boots.

Anna's heart pounded so loud, her ears rang. If Ethan said anything else, she didn't hear it. Abruptly, he turned on his heels and strode off toward the horse corrals and barn. On weak and shaky legs, Anna leaned against the cabin door. She swiped a trembling hand across her face and sucked in several breaths of air to calm her nerves.

Renewed anger surged through her. How dare he speak to her in such a rude manner? She'd made an honest mistake. Granted, getting doused with dirty water couldn't have been a pleasant experience, but he didn't have to continue acting in such a hard-headed fashion, especially since she'd apologized.

Anna shook her head. Her limbs were still shaky as she made her way from the main cabin to the one she'd called home since last autumn. She scoffed. Home? Nothing could be further from the truth.

She fumbled with the latch on the cabin door and stumbled into the dark interior. Tears blurred her vision. She didn't bother to light a lantern, and sank onto her bunk. For all the beauty to be found in this wilderness valley, there was no feeling of home here. An overwhelming sense of loneliness gripped her and she curled into a ball, allowing her emotions to get the better of her.

Chapter Two

Once he'd unbuckled his hunting belt, Ethan yanked the ends of his cotton shirt free from his britches. In his haste to strip the wet material from his body, he all but tore the buttons off. He'd endured worse pranks from his brothers over the years, but getting a bucket of muddy water tossed at him by a woman was a first. He stood in the dark barn, a cold blast of air hitting him. Although the days had definitely warmed and spring had fully arrived in the valley, a soaked shirt against his skin sent a shiver through him.

He hadn't planned on a dip in the creek today, but he might as well wash off more than just the grime on his face. The cold water might be exactly what he needed to douse his foul mood.

Ethan's eyes darted to the barn door in the direction of the cabin. Why had he let that female scare him away? His change of clothes was under his bunk, not in the barn. If he went to the creek now, he'd have nothing clean and dry to put on.

Blast that woman!

The muscles along his jaw tightened to the point of making his teeth hurt. He'd had to get away from her. For months, he hadn't had a moment's peace. Not since his brother, Nathaniel, had brought a wife and her horde of siblings with her. And Anna Porter.

As much as he'd tried not to notice, her soft smile and warm eyes had haunted him relentlessly over the long winter months, even when she wasn't around. The cabin he shared with his twin brothers and old Harley had become something more than simply a place to get out of the weather or a warm place to sleep at night.

Anna Porter had transformed the shabby lodge into a home through her unwavering persistence to keep it clean and tidy, and her resolve to make sure everyone was well-fed with her good cooking. His hand unintentionally went to rub at his stomach. He hadn't eaten better since . . .

Ethan yanked his hand away and bunched up the shirt he clutched. He scraped it across the whiskers on his face while cursing the woman's name. Her subtle feminine touches were everywhere, from the curtain that separated his sleeping area from the rest of the cabin to her work apron she always left hanging on the peg on the wall.

He ran a hand through his disheveled hair. His eyes wandered down his wet britches, then to the rim of mud around his boots. Anna Porter's scolding had rung true. He wouldn't have removed his boots before entering the cabin. Before she'd come along and disrupted his orderly life, no one had cared about mud on the floor or grease and dust building up on the mantel. She brought back too many old memories that he'd tried to forget.

The barn door creaked on its hinges. Ethan tensed. He squinted toward the golden stream of light interrupted by a man's silhouette.

"Did your horse drop you in the mud?"

Travis, one of the twins, wore a bright smile as he scrutinized Ethan's appearance.

"Something like that," Ethan growled.

Trevor, the other twin, appeared behind his brother, wearing the same perplexed look.

"Thought you was headed to the cabin. Patrick told me he saw you going that way." Trevor exchanged a look with his brother.

"Changed my mind and thought I'd get cleaned up first."

Travis snorted. "Cleaned up for what? A visit from the Osbornes never gave you cause to get gussied up before.

11

I'm already bracing myself for Aimee taking us to task for our appearance, but I never thought you'd toe the line before she's even here. Besides, the horse trough is empty. We ain't filled it, yet." He pointed to the old dugout log lining the back wall of the barn that served as a watering trough for the horses during the coldest days in winter.

Ethan's eyes went from one brother to the next. The Osbornes were coming to visit? Finally, someone he actually looked forward to seeing. Lucas Walker's social call earlier had been as annoying as having the women folk here in the valley. He respected Lucas' father, Alex Walker, as much as he did Harley and Daniel Osborne, but Alex's youngest son was worse than Travis and Trevor combined when it came to causing mischief or doing something foolish. At least he hadn't stayed long this time. The Osbornes would be a welcome change of pace.

Even for her advanced age, Aimee Osborne was a force to be reckoned with, just like her trapper husband. Her name throughout the mountains was as well-known as Daniel's. The legendary mountain man was respected by his peers and feared by his enemies, yet loved and revered by the native people as well as white men. As a healer with extraordinary knowledge, Aimee wasn't like other women who didn't belong in the wilderness. Ethan worked his jaw muscles. Women like Anna Porter, for instance.

"I'd appreciate it if you'd go to the cabin and fetch my clean shirt from under my bunk, Trev." Ethan nodded toward the barn door. "And some soap and a towel."

Travis' eyes shot up, then darted to his twin. "He wants you to fetch him some clean clothes, Trev." A wide smile passed over his face before his gaze went back to Ethan. Travis cocked his head to the side, squinting as he peered at him. "Ethan don't want to go to the cabin for some reason. It wasn't your horse that tossed you in the mud, was it?"

"Get out of here, Travis, and mind your own business before I knock some sense into your fool head. Don't you have wood to chop or something?" He'd always ignored his brothers and their goading, but he'd never hear the end of it if the twins found out he'd had a bucket of mud tossed at him. No doubt they'd find out soon enough, but he was in no mood to deal with his brothers at the moment.

"I'll get your clothes, Ethan." Trevor eyed him with a searching look. He was always the more sensible one, unlike Travis, who liked to stir up trouble. Trevor stared at him for another moment, then headed out of the barn.

"And make sure you take your boots off before you walk in, so you don't track mud into the cabin." Ethan called after him, then cursed the instant the words were out.

Travis stared at him, his eyes wider than a barn owl's. He stepped closer, and leaned forward. "Are you feverish? Since when have you cared if the floors were clean or dirty?"

Ethan scowled. "I've always cared. And you two should care a little more about the roof over your heads, too. It's time you acted a bit more grown up, don't you think? Especially you, Travis."

Travis laughed. "You've been telling us that since we was six years old, after Mama and Pop died."

Ethan's jaw clenched. He advanced on his brother. Travis held his hands out in front of him and backed up as if he was warding off an attack.

"Well then it's about time you listened," Ethan growled. "You might not remember, but Mama wouldn't have tolerated a dirty house."

"All right, all right. I'll be sure and take my boots off before I set foot in the cabin."

Ethan stared after his brothers as Travis high-tailed it out of the barn after Trevor. He faced the wall when they were out of sight and raked a hand through his hair. Cold air seeped through the half-open door, meeting his bare skin and sending a shiver up his spine. He tensed. Hell, he hadn't relaxed all winter, and it was grating on him worse each day.

The solitary life in the mountains, save for the company of his brothers and Old Harley, had suited him well over the years since they'd come to live with the mountain hermit. His secluded life had come to an abrupt halt when his brother had brought his new family home to the valley at the end of last summer. One woman would have been enough, but three more plus a young boy had worn on Ethan's nerves.

Cora, Nathaniel's wife, was a feisty woman, and tough enough to live here. She was the only one in the bunch who went out of her way to talk to him. His lips twitched. She'd even gotten a smile out of him a time or two. She was bossy and strong-minded, and just what his younger brother needed.

Her younger sibling, Caroline, wasn't as hardy as her older sister, but the youngest, Josie, was tough as nails for her quiet demeanor. She kept to herself and didn't talk to any of the men other than Harley and sometimes Nathaniel. She'd even taken to wearing britches, and Harley seemed to like her even more for it. The old codger doted on her and taught her to shoot a rifle or throw a knife every chance he got.

Then there was Anna Porter. While the other girls seemed to be making a home for themselves here in the valley, there was something about Miss Porter's demeanor that signaled she was often far away in her head. He'd caught her staring off into the distant mountains or with her eyes clouded over with sadness even when she tried to

14

smile. Although she worked as hard as, if not harder, than any of the other women, she wasn't happy here.

Ethan ground his teeth. Why did those things even catch his eye? Nathaniel had told him that he'd promised to take Anna Porter to Oregon once the weather was good enough to travel. While it meant that there would be one less woman in the valley, which was fine by him, it also meant that his brother would be absent for many months. What about Nathaniel's wife and the other women? Did he plan to leave them behind?

Ethan shrugged. It was really none of his business. The twins were often gone for weeks on end, too, and life went on as usual in the valley.

"Here are your clothes."

Ethan spun around at Trevor's words. His brother held out a fresh shirt, a towel, and even a bar of soap. He took the items from Trevor and grunted his thanks.

"What really happened to you, Ethan? There's mud in the cabin."

Ethan studied his little brother. Trevor had a good head on his shoulders, even if he let his twin influence him too much. He was quiet and responsible, and reminded him a lot of Pa, before . . . His jaw clenched.

"I don't know about any mud in the cabin," he said and moved around his brother toward the barn door. The sooner he could get to the creek and clean up, the better. Then he could wash away thoughts of Anna Porter's anguished look when he'd yelled at her.

Damn. He'd been gruff with her before when he'd told her to stay away from his personal belongings, but he'd sure put a scare in her this time. She was right. There was no reason he had to behave like such a mule, but whenever she was around, something indefinable made him act more out of sorts than with his brothers. He scoffed. Everyone called him bad-tempered, and he was fine with that. Why

15

had it bothered him this time, when Miss Porter had called him out on it?

Ethan headed for the creek that flowed behind the barn. Dense willows and cottonwoods made this a secluded spot for bathing. He stripped out of the rest of his clothes, then stepped into the water. He sucked in a quick breath when the frigid liquid touched his skin, but gritted his teeth and lathered up his arms and chest. He shot a quick glance in the direction of the main cabin. Smoke rose in a thin line from the chimney, promising warmth and a good meal as soon as he was finished cleaning up.

Truth be told, he'd enjoyed some of the domesticity that had come over the valley since the women had arrived, even if they had upset his quiet life. Before, Harley had done most of the cooking, which usually consisted of some indescribable slop of a stew in the kettle over the fire. During warm months, they simply roasted whatever meat they'd shot that day over a fire pit outside. None of them were any good at making biscuits. His mouth began to water. He hadn't tasted food as good as what Miss Porter cooked since his mother's death.

The soap slipped from his hand when his fist tightened around the slippery cake, which quickly vanished. He reached into the frigid water with both hands, fishing for the sliver of soap. Closing his fingers around it before it sank completely, Ethan quickly rinsed and left the water. He slipped into his fresh clothes and mud-caked boots, stomping on the ground to shake off the bigger chunks of dirt as he made his way to the cabin.

His mother had never stood for a dirty home, either. Everything had always been neat and orderly. Over the winter months, the more he'd watched Miss Porter work to bring some feminine touches to the cabin, the more he thought of his youth and how life had been before . . .

He scowled while his eyes scanned the distant mountains. This remote land was no place for women, especially not a woman like Anna Porter. This country made a man hard and unfeeling. It was the only way to survive here . . . and forget the past.

Ethan cleared his throat. Cora may be adapting, and so were the younger girls, but Miss Porter was different from them. She was quiet, and polite, and had no business being here.

Travis led a couple of saddle horses and a pack horse toward the corral behind the barn. Apparently their company had arrived. A woman laughed from the direction of the cabin, followed quickly by old Harley's hearty chuckle.

Aimee Osborne was easy to spot, despite her petite stature. Dressed in fringed britches and a brown cotton shirt that bunched around a wide belt at her waist, she wore her graying yellow hair in a long braid down her back. Moccasins were laced up her ankles nearly to her knees.

Next to her stood a man with shoulder-length, dark hair intermixed with streaks of silver. While he looked large and imposing next to his small wife, Daniel Osborne was no taller than the average man. What made him stand out, however, was the confident way in which he carried himself, with his shoulders back and head held high. Even for a man well into his later years, he looked imposing. The butt-end of his single-shot, black-powder rifle was propped on the ground as he held it, while his other hand rested against the lower half of his wife's back.

Harley stood with the couple, talking in boisterous tones while his hands moved wildly in front of him. He glanced in Ethan's direction at the same time Daniel turned his head. Aimee wore a wide smile when she saw him.

Ethan lengthened his strides to reach them and held out his hand to shake Daniel's, then Aimee's. Her sure grip was surprising for a woman her size and age. Before he could let go of her hand, she stepped closer, leaned up, and wrapped her free arm around his neck. Ethan bent forward to return her friendly hug.

"It's so good to see you again, Ethan. It's been a long time."

"Glad to see you're both doing well." Ethan straightened when she finally let him go, returning her smile and glancing at her husband. "What brings you this far south?"

"Daniel was getting restless after all the snow we've had this winter." Aimee laughed. "So he mentioned the idea of coming to Jackson's Hole to visit Alex and Evie Walker." Her eyes darted to her husband and her smile widened. "All it took was a comment from our son-in-law, Chase, that Daniel was getting too old to make the trip, and his mind was made up."

She stepped up to Daniel and hugged his arm. The old trapper scowled, but there was a definite twinkle and softness in his dark eyes when he returned his wife's gaze.

"We are on our way home from the other side of the Teewinots. Alex and Evie send their greetings."

"Well, next time tell that old coot Walker not ta be a stranger so long," Harley chimed in. "Jes saw his son, Lucas, a few days ago. At least that boy ain't shy about comin' fer visits."

Daniel nodded. "We passed Lucas on our way here. I told him to get home if he wanted to see his brother before he sets out for Boston."

Harley's eyes widened. "Boston? What does Joseph wanna go ta Boston fer?"

"He made a promise to an old chief of a band of Bannock that he'd find his granddaughter and bring her home."

Harley shot Ethan a perplexed look, as if he was supposed to know what was going on. Ethan shrugged. Joseph Walker had been married to a Blackfoot woman and lived with the Bannock tribe for a time, but that wouldn't explain why he'd go to Boston.

"I remember ole Alex Walker's friend, that French trapper, Laurent an' his Injun wife, got kilt by some low-down varmint. Met both of 'em once, an' their little gal. Thought she got kilt, too." Harley's eyes volleyed between Daniel and his wife. "Plum shame what happened to 'em."

"Everyone seems to think she's dead, but Joseph is determined to find out for sure. He'll be gone for most of the year," Aimee said. Her eyes went to the new cabin nestled against several tall pines about fifty yards away. "Things have changed around here, I see."

Harley laughed. "Ya don't know the half of it." He swept his hand to the cabin door. "Let's go inside and I'll get ya sommat ta drink, and we'll all catch up on news."

Ethan followed them into the cabin, bracing himself for the inevitable meeting with Anna Porter. He barely set foot across the threshold to see that the room was empty. Like Trevor had said, dried mud was smeared across the floor in front of the door, while the rest of the cabin was as neat and tidy as it had ever been.

He stepped fully into the room. Several pheasants lay on the table. The fire in the hearth burned low. Where was Miss Porter? Leaving the place less than spotless was not like her. Had he upset her enough with his callous outburst earlier that she'd clearly left in a hurry? Ethan raked his fingers through his hair and cursed under his breath.

19

Chapter Three

The cabin door squeaked on its hinges. The loud sound screeched like a high-pitched violin and was drawn out as the door slowly opened. A thin ribbon of light entered the dark cabin, becoming wider the longer the hinges squeaked. Anna sniffled and wiped the back of her hand across her face. She braced her arm on the mattress of her bed and struggled to a sitting position.

"Anna?" Cora's quiet voice called from the other side of the door. "Are you in here?"

Anna sat up fully on her bed, bringing her legs to the ground. Her time of solitude was apparently over. At least she'd had a few precious hours to herself, since there was little privacy in this small cabin. Her bunk stood against the wall next to the door while Caroline and Josie shared the small alcove partitioned off from the main room by a curtain they'd sewn and hung.

"I'm here, Cora," she acknowledged, her voice raspy. Her time of solitude and feeling sorry for herself were over. Cora's head peered around the cabin door, then she stepped fully into the room.

"Patrick told me the last time he'd seen you was at the men's cabin, washing floors. He brought you a fresh bucket of water, but that was several hours ago." She closed the door behind her, a frown on her face.

Anna swiped some hair away from her cheek and adjusted the kerchief on top of her head. She forced a smile.

"I was feeling poorly, so I thought I'd come in here and lie down for a few minutes. I must have fallen asleep."

Anna smoothed down the front of her dress, avoiding eye contact with her friend. A twinge of guilt hit her at the untruth of her words. She may have been feeling poorly after her confrontation with Ethan Wilder, but not in the sense she'd implied. And, she'd definitely not been asleep. She'd simply needed to get away from everyone for a time and wallow in her misery alone.

Cora rushed up to the bed. The mattress groaned when she sat down beside her. The frown on her face had changed to a look of worry.

"Feeling poorly?" Her hand touched Anna's forehead. "Have you been working too hard?" Cora's eyes narrowed and she tilted her head while studying her. "You should have asked for help."

Anna shook her head. She averted her eyes and glanced at her clasped hands in her lap. Blinking quickly, she forced away a new rush of tears. What on earth was going on with her? She wasn't usually this weepy. Cora's arm went around her shoulder.

"How long have you been feeling sick?" The concern in her voice was real.

Anna shook her head to avoid answering. "I'm sorry for pining the day away in here," she stammered. "I should get supper ready for the men." She moved to stand, but Cora's hand on her shoulder stopped her.

"I don't want you to worry about anything. Caroline and Josie have supper nearly finished. If you need to rest, I can bring you some food. I'm sure our visitors will understand if you don't feel like meeting them until tomorrow."

Anna lifted her head. She'd never avoided work a day in her life, even when she'd truly felt ill. Guilt nagged at her at the mention of visitors. She'd left the other cabin with a mess on the floor. The mud Patrick had tracked in still needed to be cleaned. She shook her head. It wasn't really her home, or her cabin to worry about. The men certainly didn't care, so why did it bother her so much?

"Anna?" Cora gave her a gentle nudge. "What can I get you? I could fetch Aimee Osborne, one of the guests. Wait until you meet her. You'll really like her. She's a healer, almost like a real doctor here in the wilderness. She'll know what to do to make you feel better."

Anna stiffened. She didn't need a doctor. There was nothing wrong with her that medicine would cure. "A woman doctor?"

Cora smiled. "I believe so. She sure has Caroline's attention. You know how fascinated she's been with learning how to treat wounds, ever since Trevor saved Nathaniel's life. Aimee's the one who taught him."

A quiet shudder passed through Anna. Nathaniel had nearly died from a gunshot wound on their way to the valley last summer. Neither she nor Cora had known what to do for him. If his brothers hadn't come along, he would have bled to death. Trevor had sewn him up, and Caroline had been fascinated ever since, talking about wishing she had some books on medicine she could read. Trevor had taught her some of the things he knew about plants that had medicinal properties, as well as how to treat wounds from burns or simple cuts.

"I don't need a doctor, Cora." Anna raised her eyes to her friend. She had to tell her about what had been on her mind more frequently over the last few weeks, ever since the weather had warmed. It was time she left the valley. "I just needed some time alone to think about things."

Cora studied her. A knowing look passed through her eyes. They'd been friends since they were little girls, and they knew each other well. Cora was aware that she hadn't wanted to stay in the valley, and wanted to continue on to Oregon. The subject hadn't come up all winter, but this might be a good time to finally bring it up.

Her encounter with Ethan Wilder earlier had left her more shaken up than she cared to think about. He was yet one more reason to leave. She'd made the best of the months she'd been here, even hoping to learn to like it here. Going to Oregon on her own was a daunting thought, but it had to be done.

She had to stand on her own and find that special place in the world where she'd truly feel at home. Cora had found that place in this valley, with a man by her side who loved her. Perhaps someday she might be ready to think about that again, too – a home, a good husband, and a family of her own. It wasn't going to happen here in Harley's Hole, though.

"What's going through your mind?" Cora asked, almost hesitantly. "What happened that you left the other cabin earlier? Patrick was surprised that you had gone. He said you'd asked him to bring fresh water."

Anna sat straighter. She inhaled a deep breath. She opened her mouth to speak when the door squeaked again. Caroline entered, followed by Josie. The youngest of the Hudson girls was dressed like the Wilder men, including a large hunting knife that hung from her hip. It had been a Christmas gift from Harley.

She wore her blonde hair in one long braid down her back, looking so much different than the timid young girl she'd been a year ago. Josie had definitely adjusted to living in the wilderness, even if she still didn't talk to most of the men.

"There you are," Caroline said with a bright smile on her face. "Supper is almost ready, and the men are getting restless. You know how they get when they aren't fed." Her eyes darted from her sister to Anna. "Mrs. Osborne is trying to hold them off until we return. Travis is complaining the loudest, but not even he wants to be in her bad graces, especially with her husband standing nearby with his rifle." She giggled.

Josie let out an audible huff at the mention of Travis' name. She mumbled something unappealing under her breath.

Caroline took a step closer, her eyes wide with excitement. "Ethan isn't as sullen as usual." She glanced over her shoulder, then leaned forward as if she were sharing a deep secret. "Trevor told me Ethan went to the creek to bathe and put on clean clothes and everything. Apparently the Osbornes are highly respected around here."

Anna coughed. Her hand went to cover her mouth. When she darted a hasty look at Caroline, heat crept into her face. No doubt Ethan's reason for bathing had nothing to do with their visitors. She clasped her cold hands against her cheeks, which grew hotter by the second.

"You didn't feel warm a moment ago," Cora remarked, a worried look on her face. "But you're looking rather flushed now. Maybe we should get Aimee to take a look at you."

Anna shook her head. She stood from the bed and walked across the room, keeping her back turned to the sisters.

"No, I'm fine. I feel fine," she stammered. "It's just a bit warm in here." She wrapped her arm around her middle, staring at nothing in particular. How could she possibly go out and face Ethan Wilder after what she'd done? He'd never looked angrier than when he'd stood in front of her with dirty water running down his face.

It was time to tell Cora and the others that she had to leave. Ethan had never liked any of them here. He'd had no choice but to accept Cora and her sisters and brother, but it was different for her. Anna wasn't related to them.

She couldn't hold back the quiet sob that escaped her lips. She'd been part of the family for so long, it would be nearly impossible to say goodbye.

Gentle hands wrapped around her shoulders, then the three sisters surrounded her. Each one of them looked at her with worry.

Cora was the first to speak. "What is going on, Anna? You're not acting yourself."

"I did something horrible." The words burst from Anna's mouth. She buried her face in her hands, unable to control her sobbing.

"What happened?" Cora prodded.

Caroline touched her arm. "You're incapable of doing something horrible."

Anna peered at her. "I did. He's never liked me before. He surely hates me now."

"Did what?" Cora looked more confused than before. "And who do you think hates you?"

Anna inhaled a lungful of air. Her spine stiffened as she glanced from one sister to the other. "I . . . I threw a bucket of water I used to clean the floors at Ethan." Her breath stuck in her throat.

Three pairs of eyes widened and stared at her.

"What did he do?" Caroline asked. "Even though whatever it is, no doubt he deserved it," she added without waiting for an answer.

"He didn't do anything," Anna stammered. "By the time I saw him walk up to the cabin, I'd already tossed the water at him. It hit him right in the face."

Cora coughed as if she was choking on something. "In the face?" she snorted. Her mouth opened, then widened until she laughed loudly. Caroline began to giggle, and even Josie joined them.

"Oh, how I wish I could have been there to see the look in his eyes," Cora sputtered between fits of laughter, holding her side. Caroline wiped at the tears on her face, while Josie held a hand over her mouth to conceal her giggles.

"It wasn't a pretty sight," Anna retorted.

"I'm sure it wasn't." Cora barely got the words out.

"It's not funny." Anna glared at her friends. "He yelled at me, and for good reason. I tried to apologize, but he just became angrier. He'll chase me off the minute I come near the cabin for sure."

"No, he won't," Caroline said, apparently first to compose herself. She still wore a wide smile. "When Trevor and Travis find out, you're going to be a hero."

Anna grabbed Caroline's hand, imploring her with her eyes. "Don't you dare tell them what I did. If Ethan didn't say anything, then I don't want this getting out. It'll only make things worse."

Cora forced air through her nose. "I can't keep this from Nathaniel. He's going to get the truth out of me because every time I see Ethan for the rest of today, I won't be able to stop smiling."

"It'll make things worse if you mock him about it." Anna's eyes went from Caroline to Cora.

Cora cleared her throat, then sobered. She tilted her head to study Anna's face. "Why are you letting this bother you so much? You have to admit, it's funny, especially because it's Ethan. I always look for ways to get him to stop behaving like a cantankerous mule."

"Dousing him in muddy water isn't the way to do it," Anna huffed.

Cora's ensuing smile was infectious. Anna's lips widened, eliciting another laugh from her friend.

"See, you think it's funny, too."

"It sure wasn't funny at the time," Anna conceded. For hours, she'd cried and fretted over what had happened. Cora and her sisters had immediately seen the humor in the situation. Why hadn't she seen it, too? It was rather amusing, if only it had been anyone but Ethan. His dark and cold stare still haunted her.

"I thought for sure he was going to strangle me. He's always been so disagreeable. I know he doesn't like me underfoot inside his cabin, but this time he was more than livid."

"Well, I'm sure you caught him off guard, and that's something he's not used to."

Anna scoffed. "Whether he's used to it or not, he was as rude as always. I did apologize. I certainly didn't do it on purpose." She looked from one sister to the next. She needed to explain to someone, since the person most affected would hear none of it. "The bucket was heavy, and I didn't look up when I stepped outside to toss the dirty water into the yard. I didn't see him walking up at that moment. He wanted none of my explanation."

Cora's hand was back around Anna's shoulder. She shot a quick look at her sisters. "Why don't you two go and get supper finished so that we don't keep the men waiting much longer. Anna and I will be along shortly."

Caroline exchanged a quick look with Josie, then both girls nodded and left the cabin. Clearly, they'd understood that their sister wanted to speak to Anna alone. Anna raised her brows. Why would Cora want her sisters out of earshot?

Cora took Anna's hand and led her to one of the chairs around the small table in front of the hearth. She glanced toward the door before she spoke.

"I know it had to be difficult, facing Ethan when he's mad," she said, sitting opposite her at the table. "He can seem rather cold and unfeeling, but he truly isn't like that."

Anna stared at Cora across the table. She'd wait to hear what else her friend had to say before she disagreed with her. Every encounter with Ethan Wilder over the

27

months had been anything but cordial. There wasn't a polite bone in the man's body.

"I've never told you this, because I didn't think it was important," Cora continued, "but maybe you should know. You are aware of what happened to Ethan's parents, aren't you?"

Anna nodded. "You and Nathaniel both told me. They were killed when they moved from Kentucky to settle along the Missouri. Harley found the four boys and raised them in the wilderness. You told me Nathaniel harbored a lot of guilt for not doing more to help defend his parents against the men who killed them."

Cora reached across the table and wrapped her fingers around Anna's hand. "Yes, but he's come to realize that there was nothing he could have done. He was only a boy at the time, and so were the rest of the brothers."

Anna's forehead scrunched. "What does that have to do with Ethan and his current demeanor?"

"Ethan blames himself for his parents' death. He had an argument with his father the day they were killed. Ethan wanted to go hunting, but his father told him to stay with the family. They exchanged heated words, and Ethan left. His father decided to make camp and wait for Ethan's return." She paused, smiling weakly, before she continued. "That's when they were attacked by river pirates. By the time Ethan came back, his father, mother, and little sister were murdered, and their wagon plundered. They took the mules and everything of value. Nathaniel hid in the bushes with the twins, as he'd been told to do. He told me Ethan hasn't been the same since."

Anna stared at her friend across the table. She recounted the words in her head, picturing the gruesome scene. What would have gone through Ethan's mind at returning to find his family slaughtered? He'd had a falling out with his father, and because of it, they had camped and been attacked.

"Nathaniel dealt differently with what happened," Anna whispered. Cora nodded.

"I guess Ethan felt more responsible because he's the oldest and was the one who went off after his father told him not to, and they left on bad terms." She laughed softly. "He used to be reckless like Travis."

Anna stared across the table. Nathaniel had often said that Travis put the *wild* in their last name. "I can't see that in Ethan."

"He feels he carries all the responsibility for his younger brothers, and then they taunt him about it," Cora continued. "Whether he's bitter or simply built a wall around himself, who can tell? I've been trying to get him to act less surly, and sometimes I see a hint of warmth in his eyes. I bet he's a very nice man under that cold exterior."

Anna shook her head. "You should have seen the way he looked at me when I tossed that water at him. I thought he was going to kill me."

Cora laughed again. "I'm sure he was startled by what you did. Can't blame him for that, but maybe that's just what he needed to wake up and see how his harsh demeanor affects others. He's fighting being part of a larger family. Maybe what you perceive as gruffness is actually fear."

"Fear?" Anna whispered. She understood fear, but Ethan didn't seem the type of man who feared much of anything.

"Does what I told you give you a little understanding why he might be such a closed-off man?" Cora's soft words barely reached her. Anna glanced up and nodded. Sympathy grew stronger for the man she'd considered to be nothing but callous. Perhaps she had misjudged him all this time.

It had never been like her to draw false conclusions about someone without first getting to know them. With Ethan Wilder, she'd kept her distance from the moment they'd met. Everything about his demeanor, his words, and his actions, had said to stay away. She'd never given him a chance. She'd already decided when she'd arrived in the valley that she didn't want to stay here, and she'd used Ethan's sour disposition as an added excuse.

You're no better than he is, Anna. You're afraid to form new attachments, too.

Memories filled her mind of why she'd agreed to make the trip west with Cora and her family. She hadn't wanted to remain behind, alone with her own loss and grief.

"Come to the main cabin and have supper with us, Anna. You'll like meeting the Osbornes."

Anna smiled at Cora. "Give me a minute to freshen up. My face must look a mess."

"Nothing a cool washcloth against the eyes for a few minutes won't fix." Cora stood. "I'll let everyone know you'll be there shortly." She moved around the table and gave Anna's shoulder a squeeze, then left the cabin.

Anna sat, staring at her hands in front of her. Cora's tale about Ethan might explain a lot about the eldest of the Wilder brothers, but it didn't diminish her desire to leave. Ethan Wilder's behavior was not really her concern. She had her own ghosts from her past to overcome. And the best way to deal with them was to leave, and find a place of her own where she could truly feel at home. Only then could she perhaps forget what she'd lost.

Chapter Four

Trevor carried chairs from inside the cabin and set them around the makeshift table they had erected in the yard in order to accommodate everyone for supper. Nathaniel and Travis each carried an end of a long bench to add to the chairs. A large table had already been set up using crates and wooden boards. While the main cabin at the homestead could accommodate everyone for meals, it was more comfortable eating outside now that the weather was getting warmer, and especially since there were two more people present.

"Yessir, Nathaniel's got hisself a fine wife now." Harley chortled, holding up his tin cup steaming with coffee and, no doubt, laced with a shot of whiskey. He looked in Nathaniel's direction as he approached, then turned his attention back to Daniel Osborne.

Ethan stood with them by the woodpile in the yard, a large ax in one hand. He eyed the dwindling pile of firewood stacked along the cabin. Travis clearly hadn't done the chore earlier.

"Never woulda guessed that Nate would be the first to get hisself hitched," the old man droned on. "But then, with Ethan bein' so disagreeable, it ain't no wonder. Always thought the oldest oughta get hisself a wife first."

Ethan shot Harley a dark glare. He should know better than to let the old coot goad him about the subject of marriage. They'd discussed it – or rather, Harley had discussed it – plenty of times over the last few years. Ethan wasn't going to get tugged into the same old argument again.

"Why, Nate even brung Cora's sisters. Nice buncha gals. Sure brightened up the old homestead this winter, even if someone ain't too happy they're here."

Ethan scoffed. Both Harley's and Daniel's eyes fell on him. Harley wore an amused expression while Daniel searched his face with a penetrating stare. Ethan shifted weight. He'd known Daniel Osborne for years, and the way the man could look at a person made it seem almost as if he could read someone's mind.

Luckily, his wife Aimee emerged from inside the cabin at that moment, carrying a large basket. The scent of freshly baked bread filled the air.

"This valley isn't the place for women raised in polite society, Harley, and you know it," Ethan said, cursing silently for his quick outburst.

Daniel's impassive facial expression lit up in a smile. Aimee walked past her husband at that moment and gave a quick laugh. The two of them looked at each other with knowing glances.

"And why would you say that?" Harley glared at Ethan. "I brung you and yer brothers out here when you was as green as a blade of spring grass." He swept an arm in front of him. "And look at you now."

"That's different," Ethan grumbled. His grip tightened around the ax handle. He shouldn't have opened his mouth.

"Different? How so?"

Ethan frowned. They'd had this argument countless times before, so why had he let himself get into another debate about the women with Harley, and in front of their guests no less?

"They're women," he defended even as Harley snorted. "We're men."

Harley took a long drink from his cup. "You was boys, wet-nosed boys who couldn't tell the difference atween a

32

badger and a skunk. I taught ya all how to survive. These gals can learn just the same. So can Patrick."

Josie, the youngest of the Hudson sisters came from inside the cabin carrying a Dutch oven. Her eyes darted to the old man, then shifted to Ethan and Daniel. She quickly averted her eyes. Harley waved a hand in her direction.

"Why, li'l Josie can shoot as good as Travis a'ready."

Travis, who stood by the table, scoffed for all to hear. He scowled and shot a challenging glare at the young girl. Josie set the oven on the table, and rushed back into the cabin. Daniel's lips twitched while Aimee giggled. She came up beside her husband and wrapped both her arms around one of his.

"Daniel used to think the same thing about me, Ethan." Her smile widened. "He was adamant to get me out of the mountains when we first met, isn't that right, Daniel?" She gazed up at her husband.

Daniel smiled and nodded dutifully before his eyes went to Ethan.

"My wife proved to me she was strong enough to live a life away from civilization. The greater the pull of attraction became, the more I tried to deny it and tell myself that she needed to go." His face took on a serious expression. "My stubborn attitude nearly cost me my life, and the woman I love."

Ethan smirked. He shook his head. There was no 'pull of attraction' for any of these women. All they'd done was disrupt his quiet existence.

"Cora's sisters might not mind living in this valley, but Anna Porter sure doesn't want to be here. She's already made that plain as day."

"And here I figgered you didn't pay no attention to what the women was sayin'," Harley chuckled. "If ya warn't so surly all the time, scarin' that young lady half ta death

33

every time ya cross her path, she might not wanna up an' leave."

A twinge of guilt passed through him. To ward off the feeling, he bent and grabbed for a large piece of wood, which he set on the chopping block. Swinging the ax over his head, he brought it down with more force than necessary to split the piece in half. The two pieces bounced off the block and landed several feet away. Harley chuckled. Ethan gritted his teeth and reached for another piece of wood.

"Supper's ready," Cora called. She set a large platter in the center of the table with several roasted pheasants on it.

"About time," Travis chimed. "I'm starvin'."

"You're always starving, Travis Wilder," Cora said with a laugh. She swatted his hand away when he reached for a slice of bread. "Don't you dare start until everyone's at the table."

"We been eatin' like kings since the women come to the valley," Harley said to Daniel, smacking his lips. He patted his old friend on the back and nudged him toward the table. "Cora an' her sisters shore know how ta cook a good meal, but there ain't no one who can make biscuits like Miss Anna Porter."

Ethan scanned the yard. Caroline emerged from the cabin carrying a steaming bowl. Where was Anna? Come to think of it, he hadn't seen her since he'd walked away from the cabin with mud on his face.

The look of fear in her eyes when he'd towered over her in his anger sent another dose of guilt through him. She'd covered up that fear with annoyance and had stood her ground, something she'd never done before, at least not with him.

She'd mostly avoided him, especially after the one time he'd chased her away from his bunk in the cabin when she was collecting dirty laundry. She'd had no business going through his personal things, and she'd stayed away ever since he'd told her so. His brothers and Harley might be agreeable to having a woman do their laundry, but he wanted no part in it. Keeping his distance from the woman was for the best. Except for quick greetings or general questions, she probably hadn't spoken more than five words to him in all the time she'd been here, until today when she'd told him he was rude.

Ethan looked toward the cabin door again. He shrugged. What difference did it make if Anna Porter was present? When had he wasted even a moment thinking about her? He straightened. There *had* been times when he'd caught himself thinking about her, even watching her from afar. He shook his head. He had no business thinking of Anna Porter or any other woman.

No. Every time his thoughts had drifted to her, it had been to think about how nice and orderly his life had been before she'd come to the valley. Or at least as orderly as it could be with his brothers always up to no good.

Absently, he shaved kindling from the piece of wood he still held in his hand. After supper, he'd tan Travis' hide for not getting the wood chopped. A flutter coming from the women's cabin caught his eye.

Anna Porter emerged from the cabin, her skirts swishing around her legs in the breeze. She raised her hand to her head to hold on to the thing covering her dark hair. His eyes fixed on her as if he'd never seen her before. There was something different about her that he couldn't put his finger on. He'd never noticed how she walked with her back straight and her head held high, or how the swaying of her hips made her dress rustle around her legs as if enticing him.

His eyes followed her as she approached the gathering in the yard. Ethan slid the ax down the block of wood, his focus lost on what he was doing. Faster than he could blink an eye, the sharp blade snagged on a knot in the wood, then slipped and sliced into his hand. Ethan cursed loud enough for all to hear.

He dropped the ax to grab his wrist as blood gushed from a deep cut in his palm. He gritted his teeth and cursed again. Of all the fool-headed things he'd done, he'd never cut himself with an ax blade before. His eyes shot again to Anna Porter, who'd reached the table at that moment. Her eyes, along with everyone else's, were directed at him.

Caroline gasped when she saw the hand he held up. Aimee Osborne jumped from her seat in a fluid movement that belied her age. She rushed to his side, grabbing for his wrist.

"Sit, Ethan," she commanded. Without thinking twice about it, he did as he was told, sitting on the old chopping block. She raised his hand higher over his head.

"Daniel, grab my medical pouch," she called over her shoulder. "I left it on the table in Nathaniel's cabin." Turning back to look at the injured hand, she said, "Maybe you should lie on the ground. That's quite a bleeder."

"What in tarnation did ya do that fer?" Harley called, walking over and staring down at him. He pointed at Ethan's bleeding hand. Blood continued to run down his arm, soaking the sleeve of his shirt.

"He's just looking for attention," Travis called from the table. "While the rest of us are starving."

Cora shushed him while Nathaniel reached across the table and cuffed his younger brother across the head. Travis ducked, hitting his chin against his plate and splattering greens and meat onto his lap. He jumped to his feet, knocking the chair out from under him. Travis shot Ethan a scalding look as if it was his fault that he'd dumped his food. Ethan returned his brother's scowl. Served him right.

36

Aimee tore a fringe of hide from Trevor's shirt, who'd come up beside her. She tied it around Ethan's wrist, making his hand pulse.

"Trevor, I need sugar." The older woman shot a quick glance at Ethan's brother. "Unless you know where to find a large amount of spider webs."

"Spider webs?" Caroline gaped at Aimee.

"They help stop bleeding, but I think I'd rather have sugar. It's cleaner in this case, and I don't think we'd find enough in a short amount of time."

Ethan's eyes volleyed between the two. What in tarnation were they talking about?

"I'll get the sugar," Caroline offered, and rushed into the cabin. She returned a few moments later, carrying a pewter crock.

"Hold out your hand, Ethan." Aimee Osborne didn't wait for Ethan to do as she asked. She grabbed his hand and held it palm-up, then poured some of the contents of the crock onto it. The white crystals quickly turned crimson.

"Who has a clean cloth?"

"I do. It's freshly laundered." Anna Porter stepped forward and held out a white handkerchief. It was embroidered at the corners with neat stitches resembling flowers. Ethan glanced up, meeting her gaze for a split-second before she averted her eyes. Aimee wrapped the cloth around his hand.

"I'll have to see how deep this cut is once it stops bleeding," she said, looking at him. "Then I can sew it up. For now, keep your hand above your head."

Daniel returned at that moment, carrying a leather pouch. Aimee rummaged through it, pulling out a smaller pouch. She unrolled a brown-tinted bottle wrapped in thick leather.

"There's hot water simmering over the hearth," Cora offered. "Do you need some of that?"

Aimee nodded. "Has it been boiling?"

"Yes, for quite a while earlier."

"Can you bring me a pitcher with some of the boiled water and a cup, and drop my needle and some thread in it. And if Harley has any whiskey in the house, bring some of that, too."

"I'll be right back."

Cora took the pouch Aimee handed her. The healer returned her attention to Ethan. "I can give you some laudanum for pain when I stich up the hand."

Ethan looked at her. He shook his head. "No need," he grumbled, perfectly aware that everyone's eyes were on him. If he showed any weakness by asking for something to dull the searing pain, he'd never live it down with his brothers. His eyes involuntarily drifted to Anna, who stood the furthest away. The muscles along his shoulders stiffened. If it hadn't been for her coming out of the cabin when she did and catching his eye, he wouldn't have sliced his hand open.

"Suit yourself." Aimee shook her head and threw him an indulgent smile, as if she'd received the same answer countless times before. She leaned forward, and whispered so only he could hear, "No need to prove anything to anyone here, Ethan. You won't lose the respect of your family if you choose not to be in pain."

"I'll be fine," he said between gritted teeth. Aimee nodded and straightened, no doubt knowing that his answer wouldn't change.

She inspected his wound, unwrapping the blood-soaked handkerchief from his hand. The sugar had dissolved into a runny, red substance, and dripped from his hand to the ground, revealing a gaping slice in his palm. Cora returned with a tin cup, a bowl, and a pitcher steaming with hot water, and a bottle of Harley's whiskey. Aimee poured some of the alcohol into the cup, then raised it to Ethan's hand.

"This is going to sting," she said. Before he could react, she poured the contents over his palm.

Ethan hissed, trying to pull his hand back, but Aimee held tight. She smiled. "Told you it would sting. Just trying to get it clean before I sew it up." She brought his hand closer to her face, inspecting the wound. "I can't tell, but it doesn't look like you sliced through any tendons. Can you stretch and bend your fingers?"

Ethan tentatively moved his fingers to fully open his palm. The pain intensified, as if hot needles stabbed at him repeatedly. He clenched his jaw. Aimee nodded in satisfaction.

"You may not want laudanum for when I sew you up, but you will drink some willow bark tea. It'll help with any pain later." Her stern look dared him to decline, so he simply nodded.

"Can someone brew some willow bark tea?" Aimee asked no one in particular.

"I'll do it."

Ethan's eyes narrowed when Anna stepped forward. She looked his way for a fraction of a second, then turned her gaze on Aimee.

"I have several satchels of herbs in my bag. Willow bark looks like dark wood shavings. Steep about a spoonful in a cup of hot water." She offered a smile to Anna, who nodded and reached for the leather pouch at Aimee's feet.

Without looking at Ethan, she rushed to the cabin. Ethan's eyes lingered on her retreating form. Why would she offer to help? He glanced around. Harley and Daniel sat at the table, along with Travis, who stared longingly at the food in front of him. Josie sat by herself at the far end of the table, not looking at anyone in particular.

When Cora returned with Aimee's sewing materials, Trevor and Caroline hovered around her. Aimee rinsed her hands, then glanced at Trevor.

"Pour some whiskey over my hands, please," she said, holding her needle and thread.

"Whatcha wastin' my good whiskey fer?" Harley called from the table. He looked as if an entire year's cache of animal furs had gone up in flames as he watched his whiskey drip to the ground.

Ethan grimaced, and perspiration beaded on his forehead when Aimee began to stich the wound together, but he forced his hand to remain quiet while she worked. Thankfully, she was quick and efficient. When she was done, she wrapped a bandage around his hand and wrist.

"You won't have use of your hand for about a week," she said, rinsing the blood from her own hands. "Daniel and I won't be here, but Trevor can take the stitches out in a couple of weeks. I'll leave instructions with your brother in case there is infection, but if you keep it clean, it should heal just fine."

"Much obliged to you," Ethan said. Aimee nodded, and joined Harley and her husband at the table.

"That was incredible what you did, Mrs. Osborne," Caroline said, looking at Aimee with awe. She remained close by her side, and whatever else was said was lost to Ethan.

"Can we eat now?" Travis asked. "Food's getting cold."

"Yeah, ya best eat afore ya starve, Trav," Harley chortled. He raised his cup of whiskey-laced coffee, and reached for a piece of bread. "An' someone hand me my bottle a whiskey afore it all gets spilt on the dirt."

Ethan flexed his arm but couldn't fully extend his fingers with the bandage wrapped around his palm and wrist. Of all the dumb luck, why did he have to cut his hand? He'd be useless to do much of anything for a few days.

He moved to stand when Anna emerged from the main cabin. She glanced his way, paused, then squared her shoulders and headed directly for him. Ethan groaned. He didn't want to talk to her. He owed her an apology for calling her witless earlier this afternoon, but not in front of his family and friends.

"Here's your tea. Best drink it while it's hot."

Anna held the cup out to him. Ethan stood. Having her look down at him made the back of his neck itch. He raised himself to his full height in front of her, standing several inches taller than she.

"Thanks," he mumbled, and took the cup she offered. He wrinkled his nose at the bitter smell coming from the cup. Anything medicinal never tasted good. Anna remained in front of him for several seconds. There was a silent challenge in her eyes, as if testing him to see if he would drink the contents of the cup.

He raised it to his lips, holding it out to her first in a gesture of a toast, then drained the contents in one long swallow. He shuddered at the bitter taste and the tingling feeling as the liquid went down his throat. When he lowered the cup, Anna had already stepped away with her back turned to him. She took her seat at the table next to Josie without another glance his way.

Ethan took a step forward to join everyone for supper. His stomach roiled and heat raced up his face. His body suddenly heated as if he'd stepped through steam in one of those mud pools up on the Yellowstone. Nausea slammed him with such force, he gripped at his stomach and leaned forward. He shot a quick look toward the table and Anna Porter. She glanced his way at that moment and their eyes met.

41

"You trying to poison me on top of everything else you've already done to me today, woman?" he croaked, then rushed behind the cabin toward the trees to empty his stomach contents.

Chapter Five

"I gave him some mint to chew on to soothe his stomach." Aimee Osborne emerged from the cabin. "He'll be fine in a day or two, I'm sure, but he'll probably be in some discomfort for the rest of the night." She glanced around, looking at everyone gathered around the table.

Anna shook her head. If only the ground could swallow her up. The men had all finished eating their cold supper as if nothing had happened. No one seemed too concerned for Ethan's well-being, as if it was a normal occurrence that a member of their family had almost cut off his hand and then nearly died from poisoning. Across the table from her, Travis sniggered.

"Maybe I've been going about taking Ethan down a notch or two all wrong." He grinned, nudging his chin toward Anna. "I ain't never seen him so green in the face, or willing to take to his bunk and admit he wasn't feeling well."

"You'd be howling like a baby if you'd had to endure half of what's happened to your brother today, Travis," Cora scolded.

Anna tuned out the bickering. Her plate sat in front of her, the food untouched. She'd much rather return to her cabin and try for sleep to forget about this horrible day, but she couldn't appear rude in front of the visitors, either. Besides, driven by guilt, she had to know about Ethan's condition.

She sought Aimee's eyes. "He's going to be all right, isn't he? I feel so responsible for all of this."

Aimee came up beside her and pulled up an empty chair. "Well, you certainly can't blame yourself for his injured hand." She offered an encouraging smile. "He'll be fine. His pride might be a bit wounded, but he's a man." She paused and glanced at every man sitting at the table. "None of them like to be seen as weak or vulnerable, especially in front of women or their peers, so that means pretty much all the time."

Caroline and Cora chuckled at her comment. Aimee patted Anna's hand. "I'm the one who should feel responsible. I forgot about the Indian tobacco I had in my bag. It was an easy mistake to get it mixed up with willow bark." She laughed and glanced at her husband. "I made a similar mistake once when I first came to these mountains and was learning about healing herbs, isn't that right, Daniel?"

Daniel Osborne looked her way. "I wasn't sure at the time what I had done wrong that you wanted to poison me." He smiled.

Anna's eyes widened. "What I gave Ethan is poisonous?"

Aimee shook her head. "The small amount you used in the tea won't kill him. It's called puke weed for a reason. It simply made him sick to his stomach, and he's going to sweat for a while, but he'll be fine." She chuckled. "He refused a cup of willow bark tea, though."

"Can you leave some of that puke weed here with us, Aimee?" Travis chimed in. "Ethan might need another dose whenever he gets too ornery."

"Watch it, Trav, or Anna might slip some of it into your coffee one of these days for your sass," Nathaniel said, which earned him a jab in the side from his wife.

"Is there something that can be done to help his recovery?" Anna ignored the men and their banter. Although they made a habit of teasing and goading each other, the Wilder brothers would lay down their lives if one of their own was in danger.

"His stomach needs to settle. I'm sure most of what he drank came back up. I'm more worried about his hand, to tell you the truth. Infection can set in easily, and something tells me he won't keep that bandage clean once Daniel and I leave to head home tomorrow."

"I'm sure he's already thought of a reason to hold me responsible for that, as well," Anna mumbled. At least the other men and Aimee didn't know of the earlier incident with the muddy water.

Cora coughed, which sounded suspiciously like a suppressed laugh, and Caroline joined her. Anna shot her friends a glaring look. After today, it became even more important that she leave as soon as possible. If Ethan hadn't disliked her enough already, he now thought she'd tried to poison him on purpose.

"Trevor and I will make sure he follows your instructions, Aimee," Caroline said, looking at Aimee Osborne with awe in her eyes. "I wish that someday I could be as knowledgeable as you and learn to heal people."

Aimee smiled at the young girl. "There's no reason you can't," she said. "You're about the right age to enter university, aren't you? You should consider going to medical school."

Caroline's eyes widened. She laughed nervously. "Medical school? How's that possible? A woman can go to school to be a doctor?"

"I'm sure there are women who've gone to medical school. If you're interested, I can find out for you. My son, Matthew, is a doctor in New York." She looked toward her husband, then added with a note of pride in her voice. "Our other son, Zach, recently opened his own law practice in St. Louis. He, too, might know of a college that accepts women."

Caroline's face lit up like a lightning bug. "Did you hear that, Cora? I could go to college and learn to be a doctor."

Cora nodded. "Wouldn't that be something? We can certainly talk about it if that's what really interests you."

"Oh, yes." Caroline glanced excitedly from Cora to everyone else around the table. She smiled at Trevor, who sat next to her.

Travis' twin looked at her with an unreadable expression on his face. He seemed more quiet than normal. Anna's lips twitched to suppress a smile. Trevor hid that he was smitten with Caroline well, but she'd frequently observed the way he looked at Cora's younger sister when he thought no one else was watching. Clearly, he hadn't made his feelings known to her, yet, which was for the best. They were too young for romantic notions.

A sharp pain jabbed Anna in the chest, as if a knife had been thrust into her. Hadn't she felt the stirrings of young love at about the same age as Caroline was now? She blinked and looked toward the distant mountains.

As exciting and beautiful as it was to fall in love, the pain of losing that person was unbearable. At least Caroline didn't seem to notice Trevor's adoration. It might be a good thing if she left this valley for some schooling in the east. The Wilder men lived a rough and dangerous life. Even though Cora had found a good man in Nathaniel, she'd often expressed her worry about the possibility that she might lose him to some unknown danger in the wilderness.

"Where did you go to school to become a doctor?" Caroline asked eagerly, looking at Aimee. The older woman exchanged a quick look with her husband.

"I grew up in New York." Her response seemed a bit vague.

"I ain't never heard of a woman going to school and becoming a doctor before," Travis chimed in.

"That's because you're thick-headed like a mule, Travis Wilder," Josie mumbled under her breath next to Anna. She kept her head down, looking at her hands in her lap. No one seemed to have heard her. Anna's brows rose while she studied the girl. Josie usually kept quiet when the men gathered at the table. Her mistrust of most men hadn't gone away after the horrific ordeal she'd endured nearly a year ago.

Anna shifted in her seat. Perhaps now was as good a time as any to speak to Nathaniel about taking her to Oregon. Before she faced him, Cora stood from the table and cleared her throat.

"Since we're all here together," she said, looking from one person to the next and moving to stand behind Nathaniel's chair. She put her hand on her husband's shoulder, smiling down at him. He returned her smile and even winked at her when their eyes met. The love between them had only grown stronger over the months since they'd been married.

"Well, since most of us are together," Cora corrected, glancing at the empty chair Ethan would have occupied, "Nathaniel and I have an announcement."

"You two decided to call it quits and go your separate ways?" Travis called, a wide grin on his face. He cuffed Nathaniel on the arm. "Had enough of being hitched and tied down? Now that the weather's cleared, we can go explore the mountains, Nate. Lucas wants to go buffalo hunting on the plains. We should join him."

"I don't think so." Nathaniel chuckled. "I ain't ever letting go of the most important person in my life." He placed his hand over his wife's. Anyone could see the love he had in his eyes for Cora. After their tumultuous beginnings, there was nothing they couldn't overcome.

47

Anna sighed. She'd have to wait for Cora to finish speaking before approaching Nathaniel.

"Well, let's hear it," Harley called out. "We're all waitin' fer the news."

Cora looked at the old trapper, her smile widening. "Nathaniel and I . . ." She hesitated, then straightened, and raised her chin. "I'm in the family way."

* * * * *

Anna set aside the last of the dirty supper dishes she'd washed. Since she hadn't helped fix supper, she'd insisted on doing the cleanup. The sun had set a while ago, but everyone had remained in the yard, sitting around the table, talking and laughing. Trevor and Travis had built a fire in the pit that was used to cook large game. It illuminated the entire area in front of the main cabin. Daniel and Harley retold stories of their earlier years trapping the mountains of the Yellowstone country.

Cora reached for the last plate that needed to be dried.

Anna set aside her wet dishrag and wrapped her arms around her friend's neck. "I'm so happy for you, Cora." They both cried with joy, clinging to each other.

"I can't believe this is happening, that I've found so much happiness in my life. Last year, the world didn't look so bright, for any of us."

Anna nodded at Cora's words. That familiar stabbing pain pierced her heart again. A little over a year ago, her world had shattered into pieces. She'd never told anyone, not even Cora, about the depth of her grief. She'd tried to put it behind her and move on. Some days were easier than others, but she'd managed to conceal her broken heart well.

48

"I'd best get the dishes put away." Anna pulled away from her friend. "You should sit with your husband. He's making eyes at me as if I'm about to steal you away."

"I'll help," Cora offered.

"No, you won't. I didn't help with supper, so I'm finishing the cleanup."

Anna wiped her wet hands on a towel. She smiled at her friend to hide the turmoil inside her. She'd never begrudge Cora her happiness, but today the emptiness in her heart seemed wider than before.

She'd been prepared to ask Nathaniel about taking her to Oregon as he'd promised last summer, but how could she even bring up the subject now? Anna could never ask him to leave Cora for an extended length of time, now that she was expecting. Perhaps he could at least take her to Fort Hall. If not, she might even consider asking the twins. From the old trading post, she'd simply have to find a wagon company coming through that might be willing to let her join up with them, even without a male escorting her.

Anna picked up the plates and carried them to the cabin. Her heart sped up as she opened the door. Tiptoeing inside the dark space, she placed the dishes on the table as quietly as possible. Ethan hadn't made an appearance after Aimee had urged him to rest in his bunk. Hopefully, for his own sake, he would have a restful night.

The thought had barely crossed her mind, when a low moan came from behind the curtain of Ethan's sleeping area, followed by a rustling of blankets and a shuffle of feet on the wooden floor. Anna spun around. Ethan emerged from behind the curtain. He was bare from the waist up, his sweat-covered skin glistening in the golden glow of the lantern that flickered on the table. He stopped in his tracks when he glanced up.

Anna held her breath. She forced her eyes to his face rather than allowing them to travel lower, but it was difficult to ignore the well-sculpted man standing in front of her. Even though he stood slightly hunched over, his face pale and his eyes clouded with pain and discomfort, he was intimidating.

Heat crept up her neck and into her cheeks. "I thought you'd be asleep," she stammered. "I didn't intend to disturb you." She gripped the dishrag in her hand, coiling it into a tight rope.

"I need some water," he rasped, nudging his chin toward the pitcher on the counter by the hearth.

Anna moved to lift a tin mug from the shelf. Her hand trembled when she poured water into it.

"I wasn't asking you to bring it to me," he said when she handed Ethan the mug. He reached for it with his bandaged hand, then clearly thought better of it, lifting his right hand instead. His fingers grazed hers as he gripped the mug. Anna snatched her hand away, an odd jolt rushing through her from the contact.

"I know you weren't," she snapped. "I was simply trying to be helpful."

A low rumble that could have been a chuckle erupted from Ethan's chest. "That seems to be your problem, don't it?"

Anna's forehead scrunched. "What seems to be my problem, Mr. Wilder?"

"You're always so helpful."

Her spine stiffened. Even while feeling unwell, he had to be rude. His dark gaze roamed over her face, lingering on her eyes. The flickering of the lantern cast shadows over his form, making the scowl on his face appear even more ominous.

"I hope you have a restful night, Mr. Wilder." Anna skirted around him to get to the door. "Perhaps tomorrow, you'll be well enough again that feeling poorly can't be an excuse for your sour disposition." She should apologize for her mistake earlier with the tea that had made him sick, but his continued surly attitude only left her wanting to get away from him.

Anna glared at him one final time, then stepped quickly from the cabin. She blinked back the sting of tears and ignored the trembling of her hands and legs as she rushed away from the cabin. She slowed her strides to give an outward appearance that all was well while on the inside her body trembled with a mixture of anger and despair.

Cora came up to her, heading her off as she was about to excuse herself and go to her cabin. It was time to find the solitude of her bed, and perhaps forget this awful day had ever happened.

"Anna? Is everything all right?"

Anna stopped to face her friend. She was done pretending. Nothing was all right.

"No." Her voice cracked. "Things aren't all right. And apparently I can't do anything right, either." She sucked in a quick breath.

Anna glanced around. Everyone still sat around the table. Daniel spoke with Nathaniel, Travis, and Harley, while Caroline was in conversation with Aimee. Patrick sat between the two old mountain men, his eyes glued to Daniel. Only Trevor and Josie sat by themselves, apparently deep in their own thoughts. Anna shot a quick glance toward the cabin she'd left a moment ago.

"I wanted to say something earlier, but now I can't possibly ask."

"Ask what?" Cora reached her hand out to touch Anna's shoulder.

Anna forced a smile. "You've been my best friend for most of my life, Cora. I tried, I really did, to make a life here." She shook her head. "I simply can't do it. It's time I think about leaving, and continue on to Oregon. I need to find my own place in the world."

"Anna," Cora whispered her name, sadness clouding her eyes. "I was hoping you'd stay here with us, since you haven't mentioned leaving."

"I love you, Caroline, Josie, and Patrick, but there's an emptiness inside me, and a calling for something I can't even name. I have to find out what that is. Please understand."

Cora nodded. Her smile was strained. "I do understand," she whispered. "When we came here, you agreed to stay the winter, and that if you still wanted to leave come spring, we'd make sure you got to Oregon."

"I could never impose on Nathaniel to escort me to Oregon like he promised. Not with you having a baby on the way. You need your husband here with you."

"We'll think of something," Cora said. "You know I won't stand in your way, even if it pains me to see you go, and I'll talk to Nathaniel."

Harley stepped up to them at that moment. "Couldn't help but overhear," he said, looking at Anna and running his fingers through his beard. "I hate ta see ya leave us, Anna, but sometimes a person's gotta do what they think is right fer themselves."

He glanced toward the cabin, then smiled. He cleared his throat, and in a loud voice that everyone around him could hear said, "If yer sure you want to head off to Oreegun, I think the right man to take ya an' make sure ya get there safely is Ethan. Far as I can figure, he ain't got nothin' better ta do." He raised his chin, and nodded in the direction of the cabin. "Ain't that right, Ethan?"

Anna shook her head in protest. Her eyes followed old Harley's movement and her mouth fell open. Standing in the open doorframe, staring at her, was Ethan Wilder.

Chapter Six

Ethan sat on his bunk and slipped an arm though the sleeve of his shirt. His stomach growled while his dry tongue stuck to the roof of his mouth. At least the nausea was gone, even though pain still jabbed his gut like hot needles. He stood, grimacing when his bandaged hand bumped into the wooden corner of the bed.

Which hurt worse – his stomach or his injured hand? They seemed to have traded off tormenting him during the night. He scowled. Nothing had plagued him more than the look on Anna's face last evening when she'd offered him the glass of water and he'd made that snide remark to her about always being so helpful.

Remorse and even a hint of pity had been clearly written in her eyes, yet she'd bristled when he'd acted like the mule his brothers so often accused him of being. It was just as well. He didn't need her damn pity. Wasn't it because of her that he'd been feeling sicker than a dog?

Ethan fumbled with the buttons of his shirt. Aimee Osborne had wrapped the confining bandage around his hand so effectively, his fingers couldn't move to slip the button through the hole. After several attempts, he gave up. His left hand was useless at the moment. There hadn't been a time in his life when he'd felt like such an invalid. The muscles along his jaw tightened instantly before he'd even finished that thought.

There had been one day in his life when he'd felt even more helpless, and it had nothing to do with a physical injury. He might not have been an invalid as a fifteen-year-old boy, but the day he'd found his parents slaughtered had changed his entire life, and he'd never felt as helpless before or since. A dozen years had passed since that horrible day, and it was still as vivid in his mind now as if it had happened yesterday.

Ethan glanced at his hand. He'd gladly slice off his entire arm if he could alter the course of events of that day. It had changed him as a person, had made him hard and unfeeling, because he never wanted to experience that kind of pain or guilt again. Voices from his past echoed in his head – the voice of a hot-tempered youth yelling at his father that he hated him for telling him what to do, then the voice of his mother calling to him that he surely didn't mean his disrespectful words when he'd stormed from camp. He'd ignored her, and the baby sister he'd left sitting in the dirt. She'd cried, repeatedly calling "Ean, no go," because she'd been too young to say his name correctly.

Ethan wiped a hand over his damp face. Those had been the last moments he'd spent with his folks alive. When he'd returned to their camp, their wagon had been in flames and the bodies of his parents and baby sister lay on the ground, bathed in their own blood, and lifeless. His three younger brothers hid in the bushes, far enough away not to have been discovered.

Anger had been Ethan's first reaction. The guilt followed later. When he'd lain his little sister in her grave, his heart had turned to ice. She'd adored him, and he'd ignored her on her final day. She shouldn't have died in the wilderness. She shouldn't have even been in the wilderness. Why had his father brought his family to an unsettled place along the Missouri, away from the safety of a settlement and other people?

Self-loathing and a steely resolve had steadily grown inside him. He'd felt weak and helpless, and consumed by guilt, making him rigid and unfeeling. Had he not been so impulsive, he could have done something to save his folks. He should have been there, rather than running through the woods, trying to prove he was no longer a young boy who had to listen to his folks.

Ethan shook his head. Frustration made the muscles along his neck and shoulders taut. He would never be like his father and risk the lives of a wife and family in the wilderness.

When Harley had found him and his brothers, he'd gladly made the decision to go with him into uncharted mountains. Here it was easier to forget everything he'd ever loved. He'd learned how to survive on his own and, aside from his brothers and Harley, would never have to face the kind of loss he'd experienced before.

Ethan raked the fingers of his good hand through his hair. Sweat bathed his face again, like it had most of the night. The voices of his past hadn't tormented him this much in a long time, but they'd been a constant presence during the long hours of the night while his body battled to rid itself of the puke weed he'd ingested.

The mint Aimee Osborne had given him had soothed his stomach a little, but then the pain in his hand had taken over. Any water he'd drunk to quench his raging thirst had come up again moments later. Anger at Anna Porter for giving him the vile drink in the first place had teetered with guilt over his behavior where she was concerned. Truthfully, none of what she'd done to him yesterday had been on purpose, yet he'd made her feel as if she'd caused the injury to his hand, as well as acting like she'd deliberately switched the herbs for the tea Aimee had wanted him to drink.

The cabin door creaked open, followed by loud voices. Aimee Osborne laughed along with Harley.

"You'll have to come visit soon, Harley. Sarah and Chase would be happy to see you."

"I bet them young'uns they got are growin' up mighty fast." Harley chuckled. "Chase done good, raisin' four girls. Bet he's glad he's got hisself a son, though." He cleared his throat, then asked, "Gotta be hard for Sam, raisin' his little boy without a ma."

There was a slight pause before Aimee answered. "He takes Josh to spend a lot of time with his Shoshone relatives. Sam is raising him to know both his white and Indian heritage."

"Good thing, too," Harley said. "I ain't shore if I done the right thing by takin' my boys away from all they knowd an' raisin' 'em here in the mountains after their folks died. Mebe I oughta have took 'em back ta where they come from. Trevor's real smart. He coulda done good with some book learnin'." He coughed. "They all growd up ta respect the mountains, but that's all they know now."

Chairs scraped across the floor, and someone poured liquid into a cup. Harley's voice lowered when he spoke again. "Ethan's growin' more surly every year, blamin' hisself for what happened to his folks an' not lettin' go. He needs a family of his own ta move on, but he don't listen ta what I say. "

"We all do the best we can for our kids, Harley." Aimee's voice had lowered, too. "You raised them well. They're grown men, and have to make their own choices. Nathaniel has a nice family. Cora's a real delight, and so are her sisters and brother."

Harley chuckled again. "They shore do brighten up the valley. Jes wish Anna warn't leavin'. She's lonely an' somethin's eatin' at her that she don't wanna talk about. She needs a man, an' Ethan needs a woman, but neither one of 'em see it."

Being privy to the conversation between Aimee and Harley bristled the hair at the back of Ethan's neck. The old man had made it no secret for years that he wanted Ethan to find a wife. Now he was trying to match him up with Anna Porter? The thought was almost laughable.

Harley had it all wrong. Ethan didn't want, or need, a family. Even if getting hitched was ever something on his mind, which it wasn't, Anna Porter was the last woman he'd ever consider. He'd sealed off his heart a long time ago, and that's how it would remain.

Good thing Anna had plans to leave the valley. At least the woman had some sense. She didn't belong here. She was too fragile and soft to live in this environment. For that very reason, he hadn't even responded to Harley the night before when the old man had suggested he take Anna to Oregon. He was not going to be held responsible for her safety. What if something happened to her along the way? He wasn't going down that road again.

Aimee laughed. "Your matchmaking efforts haven't paid off, have they? You can't force something like that, Harley," she added softly. "I hope Anna finds what she's looking for in Oregon. I was miserable when Daniel's father forced me out of the mountains, thinking he was doing what was best for me. If Daniel hadn't found me again, my life would have been completely different."

"Good thing ya come back," Harley said. "Many men woulda gone under if ya hadn't been around with yer healin' skills."

"I can't imagine living anywhere else."

Feet shuffled across the floor, and the kettle used to heat water clanked. Aimee's voice drew closer to where Ethan still stood next to his bunk. He fumbled with his boots and pushed aside the curtain, stepping into the main room.

"Oh, good. You're awake," Aimee said brightly, stirring a spoon in a cup at the table. She stopped and walked up to him. "How's the hand?"

"All right." Ethan pushed his foot fully into his boot and straightened. "When am I gonna have full use of it again?"

Aimee scrutinized him, her eyes wandering to his unbuttoned shirt. A knowing smile passed over her lips.

"The less you use it for a while, the faster it will heal. I put a thick bandage on it to keep your hand as protected and immobile as possible. If you follow my instructions, it should be better again in a couple of weeks."

Ethan cursed silently. How was he going to get any work done for two weeks with only one hand? He couldn't even button his shirt. Aimee stepped up to him, as if she'd read his mind. She reached for the buttons on his shirt, but he shot her a look, silently telling her he didn't want her help. He'd known Aimee Osborne for years, but her motherly gesture at the moment only added salt to his wounds.

"You're going to have to swallow your pride and let people help you," she said with an indulgent smile and dropped her hands. "I know it's hard, but your family cares about you, and a few days of being at their mercy and letting them do things for you is better than a lifetime of a useless hand." She reached up and patted his arm. "I left a pouch with willow bark and some mint on the table." She pointed to the cup at the table. "There's tea ready for you and Caroline and Trevor know how to change your bandage. Listen to them." She jabbed her finger into his chest.

Ethan nodded wordlessly. She was right, but he didn't have to like it.

She glared up at him. For her small stature, Aimee Osborne was an imposing woman. "Get some rest today. You still don't look well. Keep chewing mint, and drink as much water as your stomach can handle."

"You leaving?"

Aimee nodded. "I just wanted to check on you before we go. Daniel's getting the horses ready. We've already said our goodbyes to everyone. As much as he wanted to get away from home for a while, he's anxious to get back."

Ethan followed her out of the cabin. Daniel Osborne sat on his horse, his flintlock draped across his lap. The old trapper smiled at his wife, then raised his hand in a gesture of farewell.

He nodded at Harley, who helped Aimee mount her horse, then turned his attention to Ethan. "Come visit when you can," he said. "Sam and Chase will be glad for the company."

Ethan raised his bandaged hand. "Once I'm healed, I just might do that. Like you, it'll do me some good to get away from this valley for a while." He shot a quick look at Harley, who chuckled.

"If'n ya go ta Oreegun, ya'll get away fer a while, too," the old codger mumbled.

Ethan scowled and shook his head. Once Aimee and Daniel were out of sight, he headed back into the cabin without another word to Harley. He wasn't going to let the old man corner him into another discussion about marriage and family again. Taking some of the mint the healer had left, he kicked off his boots and crawled back under the covers of his bed.

Moments later – or was it hours? – Ethan startled awake, but his eyes remained closed to hold on to the images from his dream for a few moments longer. He moved his head from side to side and threw off the covers. Crisp air hit his sweat-soaked torso, cooling his heated body. He sucked in several quick breaths and wiped his hand across his damp face.

He relaxed his head against his pillow. Images from his disturbing dream faded, but the memory lingered. His mother had called to him, begging him not to walk away.

"Don't make the same mistake again." He'd turned to look at her. She'd smiled at him. Ethan had reached for her hand, but he'd been too far away. The more he'd tried to grasp for her, the further away she'd moved. She'd shaken her head, then had pointed at another woman next to her.

"Don't turn your back this time." His mother's voice echoed in his head, while pointing at the dark-haired woman standing beside her. Ethan had looked at her, confused. She'd raised her head. Anna Porter, with her sad eyes, smiling that soft, enticing smile.

"Would you like some tea?" she'd asked, her words sounding hollow and far away.

"Why are you doing this to me?" he grumbled.

Ethan opened his eyes. He blinked, then frowned. Standing over him was the woman from his dream. Not his mother, but Anna Porter. She didn't smile, as her eyes darted from his chest to his face.

"Doing what? I heard you mumble in your sleep and came to see if you were all right. Would you like some tea?"

Ethan groaned and shifted, then sat up fully in his bunk. He threw his legs over the side, forcing Anna to take a step back.

"I made some meat broth, if you think your stomach is well enough to handle some nourishment."

Ethan ran his hand through his hair. He gritted his teeth and pushed his disturbing dream from his mind. Then he looked up at Anna.

"I promise, I didn't put anything unbecoming in the broth, or the tea." She offered a tentative smile. Her face transformed instantly in front of him. Her soft brown eyes held a hint of hesitation, but there was patience and determination, and none of the wariness he'd seen the day before. Ethan blinked again to focus. What the hell was she trying to do to him, looking at him like that?

"What do you want, Miss Porter?" he growled. "Did Harley put you up to this? You think you can sweet-talk me into taking you to Oregon?"

She frowned and a spark of anger pushed aside the softness she'd shown a moment ago. Her hand shot to her hip. Her mouth opened, then she clamped her lips together. Her chest heaved when she inhaled deeply through her nose and she closed her eyes for a split-second. When she opened them again, the anger was gone, replaced by hurt.

"I'll ask your brother or Caroline to look in on you, Mr. Wilder. Clearly, your disposition hasn't yet improved," she said, her voice calm and even.

She spun on her heels and stepped into the main room of the cabin. Without looking back at him, she pointed to the foot of his bed.

"I found your dirty clothes in the barn. I know you don't like anyone touching your belongings, so forgive me for having taken it upon myself to wash them, since I feel responsible for getting them dirty in the first place." She pulled the curtain closed behind her with a swift yank and disappeared from view.

Ethan cursed under his breath and sprang to his feet. Stars swirled in front of his eyes, and he swayed to steady himself, waiting for the dizziness to subside. Damn him for his impulsive rush to judge, and damn the woman for being so infuriatingly calm and genuinely caring. If she'd simply have a temper, he'd have something to latch onto and fight back, but her quiet demeanor left him at a complete disadvantage. There was no valid excuse to be angry with her.

Ethan stared at the curtain. His mother's words from his dream haunted him. *Don't turn your back this time.* What did she mean by that? That he shouldn't turn his back on Anna Porter, and offer to take her away from the valley to Oregon?

Pushing aside the curtain, he stepped into the room just as Anna reached for the door handle to leave the cabin.

"Miss Porter," he called. Her back stiffened but she didn't stop. Ethan rushed to her and reached for her arm before she could leave. She spun to face him, looking up at him with wide eyes.

Ethan stared at her. Details about her face that he'd never noticed before came into focus. He'd never stood this close to her, not even yesterday after the muddy-water incident. Her skin looked smooth as silk, provoking an irrational need to touch her cheek. Good thing his hand was still wrapped around her arm and the other was bandaged or he might have given in to the impulse. Several freckles sprinkled her nose, probably from spending too much time out in the sun. Her amber eyes mirrored her soft and tender heart. Damned if they weren't melting away the ice that enveloped his own.

"Has it ever occurred to you, Mr. Wilder, that sometimes people might do things simply to be kind to someone else, without wanting something in return? The truth is, you are the last person I would impose upon to escort me to Oregon or anywhere else, for that matter." She pulled her arm away and stepped outside.

Ethan clenched his jaw. "Miss Porter, I owe you an apology."

Chapter Seven

"He apologized?"

Cora's eyes widened at the same time a smile brightened her face. She set aside the wool shirt she held in her hand and shifted in her seat at the table in her cabin. A soft chuckle passed from her lips and she shook her head. "And you accepted?"

"Of course I accepted." Anna concentrated on her sewing, having already pricked her finger once with the sharp needle. Her stitches, which were usually neat and even, were barely passable this time. Good thing she was simply mending one of Travis' socks.

Her second encounter with Ethan Wilder in just as many days was still too unsettling. She'd chosen to eat supper with Josie in their cabin the night before, rather than with Cora and the Wilder men, so she hadn't seen him since he'd told her he'd treated her unfairly.

"What did he say?" Cora prodded, an eager look on her face.

Anna pulled the needle through the sock, careful to stay away from her thumb. She shrugged. Her eyes lifted to Josie, who sat quietly at the other end of the table, cleaning her rifle.

"He said he had no cause to blame me for the mix-up with the herbs, and he was sorry for calling me witless when I tossed the water at him. Then he thanked me for washing his clothes."

Cora's smile widened. "I suppose for Ethan, that's quite an apology. I knew that he wasn't the ogre everyone makes him out to be." She leaned forward in her chair. "Then what happened?"

Anna paused in her work. She glanced at her friend. Her forehead scrunched. "What do you mean? Nothing happened. I accepted his apology and left."

"He didn't say anything else?" Cora's brows rose, as if she was expecting a more elaborate answer.

Anna shook her head. "No. I was ready to walk out of the cabin, since he woke in a bad mood. I believe he may have thought I was someone else for a moment, the way he looked at me before he fully came to his senses. I only went to the cabin to bring him some broth and his clothes."

She'd heard a quiet moan from his bunk when she'd come to the cabin. The curtain separating his area from the main room had been left open and she'd seen him toss in his bed. He'd even reached his hand out to someone who wasn't there.

Unsure of what to do, Anna had gone to check on him since no one else was in the cabin. Sweat had covered his face and torso, and she'd almost left to find Trevor when he'd woken and stared up at her. Offering him some tea had been the first thing to come to her mind at that moment.

Cora chuckled. "I thought Caroline and Trevor were in charge of Ethan's recovery."

Anna blew air from her mouth. "I still feel responsible about what happened to him. After all, I gave him the wrong tea that made him sick. That had to be awful, especially after the accident with his hand." She glanced at her lap to avoid eye contact with Cora. "I thought a lot about what you told me, about what happened to Ethan's family. It doesn't excuse his behavior, but at least I can understand it a little better. I truly think he's closed himself off from everyone for so long, he doesn't know how to be any other way." She ventured a glance at her friend.

Cora smiled, staring at her as if she could read her mind.

"What?" Heat crept up Anna's neck and into her cheeks. The reaction to Cora's knowing smile was unexpected. She hadn't done anything improper. She'd simply wanted to ease her guilt and make sure that Ethan was all right. She couldn't have known that he'd be asleep in his bunk, or that the curtain had been pulled back, letting her see him a second time without his shirt on.

The heat in her cheeks grew in intensity. Anna sat straighter in her chair. Although Cora knew her well, she wasn't a mind reader. She couldn't have guessed at the images that lingered in her thoughts.

Besides, over the last two days, she'd been in confrontation with Ethan more often than the entire time she'd been in the valley. It had also been during these last few days that a deeper understanding of the reclusive man had surfaced, at least in her mind, thanks to what Cora had told her about him. She'd known about what had happened to the brothers' parents through Nathaniel, but it had never occurred to her that Ethan would harbor lingering guilt over what had happened.

The way he'd looked at her when he'd offered his apology had been rather unsettling. More unsettling, in fact, than when he'd towered over her and yelled at her. His eyes had always seemed so cold, yet there had almost been a spark of tenderness in them this time, completely transforming his features. He had been so out of character from the hardened man he tried to portray around the rest of his family.

"You're acting more like the Anna I know - always trying to find good in people." Cora reached a hand across the table to touch Anna's arm. She glanced up to meet her friend's smiling face, blinking away the memory of how Ethan had looked at her.

"You gave me a lot to think about the other day," Anna mumbled.

65

Over the months, she'd learned to deal with Ethan's impolite behavior by simply staying out of his way, avoiding him like most everyone else did. His apology had genuinely surprised her, and she'd been at a loss for words at how to respond. Quickly accepting his request for forgiveness, then walking away had seemed like the best thing to do. She'd lain awake last night, thinking about her misfortunate encounters with Ethan Wilder, and how his eyes had softened while he asked for her forgiveness.

"Caroline said that Ethan and Nathaniel were talking when she stopped by to check on Ethan's hand. Their conversation halted when she entered."

Anna finished her last stitch, then set the sock in her lap. There was nothing strange about that. Men didn't like to have women listen in when they talked. "It isn't unusual for them to talk, is it?"

"No, I suppose not, but maybe Nathaniel was trying to persuade Ethan to escort you at least as far as Fort Hall."

Anna shook her head and laughed. "I can't imagine Ethan Wilder taking me to Fort Hall. I think he'd rather cut off his other hand before he would make such an offer." Not that she wanted him to take her in the first place.

"Ethan's probably the safest man you could be with alone. He doesn't like anyone, so he won't bother you, either." Josie glanced up from wiping her rifle with a rag. Her eyes darted between Anna and Cora.

"I'm sure you're right," Anna said, offering a weak smile to the young girl who'd suffered so much at a man's hand. Josie had found her confidence when Nathaniel, and then Harley, had taught her to shoot. Now she was almost obsessed about her rifle. No doubt it made her feel safer. Before, she hadn't been able to defend herself against the man who had attacked her and stolen her innocence.

"You're still adamant about leaving?" Cora stared at Anna. Her face had gone serious, and sadness clouded her eyes. Anna swallowed back the sudden tightness in her throat.

"Yes. There's nothing for me here, Cora." She nodded toward Josie. "You have your family, and now a baby on the way. Perhaps Nathaniel can take me to Fort Hall, but I won't allow him to escort me all the way to Oregon. He might not be back in time for the birth of your baby. I could never impose like that."

"Can't you stay until after the baby is born?"

Anna shook her head. Tears threatened behind her eyes. Cora wasn't making her decision to leave any easier.

"That would mean another year before I can leave, and then it might be even harder to say goodbye. I have to make a fresh start for myself, Cora. There might always be something to delay my decision. Please understand. You and Caroline and Josie have been my family for so long, I think I forgot how to be my own person. I need to find my own path in life."

Cora reached for her hand, and gave it a squeeze. "And find the happiness you're looking for."

Anna dropped eye contact. The sock in her lap became blurry. "That's why I won't return to Ohio. There are too many memories there. I'm better off starting over in Oregon."

Cora's hold on her hand tightened. "How are you going to get to Oregon from Fort Hall all by yourself? No one wanted to let us join any of the wagon companies unless at least one of us was married, and even then very unwillingly." She frowned, studying Anna's face. "Are you willing to get married to a stranger just to get to Oregon?"

Anna's lips tightened. That thought had already crossed her mind. If Nathaniel had been able to take her to Oregon, she would have had a man to look out for her.

Cora might have even gone along with them. No one would have raised an eyebrow. She sighed.

Marrying a farmer on his way to Oregon might not be as bad as it seemed. Cora had been swindled, but that had been at the start of their journey. Many men lost their wives on the trek to Oregon, and needed a woman to take care of the children. As long as he was a good provider, there wouldn't need to be love involved. Besides, the thought of ever loving another man again seemed impossible.

"I don't know what I'm going to do. If I have to marry, then so be it."

"It didn't work so well for me when I simply married a man for the sake of getting to Oregon, remember?"

Anna smiled. "Yes, but then you met Nathaniel. I don't plan to find a husband for love, Cora. I just want to be content. That's the best I can hope for."

Cora stared at her for a while. She scrutinized Anna's face to the point of making her uncomfortable. After several silent seconds, Cora's eyes widened.

"Are you still mourning Franklin's death?"

A tear fell down Anna's face. She hastily swiped it away with the back of her hand and stood, turning her back.

Cora followed. She wrapped her arm around Anna's shoulder, drawing her closer. "Why didn't you ever confide in me?

"I don't know," Anna sobbed. "I thought I could move on. He was my beau since we were sixteen years old. For five years, we made plans to marry and spend the rest of our lives together."

"You were so strong and composed after he died, and so determined to leave Ohio with us. You never talked about him, and I selfishly thought you had moved on. Anna, I'm so sorry."

Anna sniffled. She pulled out of her friend's embrace and offered her a reassuring smile. "You had so much to contend with at the time, Cora. It wouldn't have been right of me to burden you with my troubles, too."

Anna shot a hasty glance at Josie, who sat watching. She set her rifle aside, and came up to Anna, offering her a hug.

"You were there for me when all I wanted to do was die, Anna. You never asked for anything in return, not even when Franklin had his accident. You were simply there, taking care of me." She glanced at her sister. "Now it's our turn to be there for you. Whatever you want to do, Cora, Caroline, and I will support you, no matter what."

Anna nodded, letting the tears flow freely, crying with her friends. Although talking about her loss was painful, it took away the deep hurt she'd kept locked up inside for so long. If Josie could overcome the horrors of what had happened to her, then she could be strong enough and move past the loss of her fiancé. She wiped her tears on a handkerchief, and straightened. Smiling, she stepped away from Josie and Cora.

"Well, I'd best get these socks back to Travis."

She stuffed her needle and thread, along with the mended socks, in her satchel that held her sewing supplies, then reached for her shawl hanging on the peg by the door.

"If you see Caroline or Trevor, can you give them this salve?" Cora handed her a round tin. "Aimee Osborne left this behind, saying it would be good to put on Ethan's hand in a few days."

Anna stuffed the tin in her satchel. Smiling at her friends, she left Cora's cabin. The newly-built home sat on a gentle rise overlooking the valley, nestled among some trees that marked the edge of the forest leading into the hills. A path led to the main cabin some hundred yards away, closer to the creek that meandered through the spring grasses past the barn. The cabin she shared with Caroline and Josie stood just beyond the corrals.

Rather than following the visible trail through the grass to the main cabin to return Travis' socks, she headed into the trees. While a good cry with Cora and Josie had eased her heavy heart somewhat, it might do her some good to be alone with her thoughts.

Even though the day was mild, Anna wrapped her shawl around her shoulders, and inhaled the fragrant, earthy scent of the lush spring meadow. The trees gave off the wonderful scent of pine, and she followed the sounds of the birds as they chirped high up in the canopies. This had been the first time she'd gone off on her own like this to explore away from the valley, and the freedom and solitude was intoxicating, allowing her mind to wander.

She'd gone walking with Franklin in the forest back home on many occasions. A stroll in the woods had been their first outing together, and it had been during one of those walks that he'd asked her to marry him. He'd been such a soft-spoken, caring person, always with a smile on his face, a kind word for his neighbors, and love in his eyes for her.

"We have to wait to be wed until I can save enough money to buy a piece of land I have my eye on. It won't be more than a few years, Anna. I'll build you a nice house, and we'll plant corn and wheat, and have a productive farm that will provide for us."

Franklin had been full of dreams without being too ambitious. He'd been such a hard worker, and despite spending all his time doing odd jobs and helping the neighboring farmers tend their land in order to earn the money for the property he'd planned to buy, he'd always found time to spend with her.

A tear rolled down her cheek. She hugged her arms around her waist, making her way through the forest. Anna

70

glanced up at the sky, which was partially obscured by the tall lodgepoles.

Why did you have to die, Franklin? It was all my fault.

Guilt crushed her chest and she hugged her shawl more firmly around herself.

"You're always so helpful." Ethan Wilder's mocking words slammed into her gut with new meaning. If she hadn't committed to helping out Cora the day of Franklin's accident, declining his invitation to eat supper with him, her fiancé might still be alive today.

"I understand, Anna. We can have supper another night."

He'd taken her hand, and with a smile on his face, had kissed her cheek. *"One thing I love about you is that you're always so helpful. Don't ever change."*

What a contrast between two men. The meaning of their exact same words to her had been so vastly different. One had said them with love in his eyes, while the other had held nothing but contempt for her. Anna adjusted her kerchief on her head. A burst of annoyance shot through her. How could she even think of Franklin and Ethan at the same time, or compare the two? No two men had ever been more different.

Anna walked faster, stumbling over the uneven ground, which was overgrown with greenery. Dead logs littered the forest floor, making navigation more difficult. The forest grew denser the further she walked and the faint trail she'd followed had long disappeared. Her skirt snagged on downed logs she had to go around or over, and the tops of the trees grew thick enough that they obstructed the sun, making it seem eerily dark all of a sudden.

She stopped, her heart beating fiercely against her ribs. She breathed as if she'd run for miles. Perspiration beaded her forehead, sending a chill down her spine when a cool breeze swept over her damp face. She glanced around, her eyes widening. Which way was back to the cabins? The forest closed around her, and nothing looked familiar.

She headed in the direction from which she'd just come, then stopped. Which way was correct? Everything looked the same. She walked past the log she'd gone around a moment ago, but had to stop again. Had that been the log, or was it the one a few feet away?

A cloud covered what little light the sun managed to send to the forest floor, instantly making everything seem even darker. How could she allow herself to get lost like this? She couldn't have gone that far from the valley that she wouldn't find her way back.

Glancing around, she studied her surroundings to see if anything was recognizable. The trees all looked the same and the forest was dense enough that she'd lost complete sense of direction. She turned in a circle, slowly studying every tree, but it was useless. Her heart sent the blood racing through her veins, making her legs and arms feel weak with growing trepidation.

The breeze swishing through the canopies sounded louder than before, and several of the tallest lodgepoles swayed and groaned in response. A woodpecker chiseled away at the trunk of a nearby tree, while ravens fluttered their wings and called to one another. The sounds they made were almost ominous.

"I am not lost," she whispered, squaring her shoulders. If she didn't return by the time dusk set in, Cora would no doubt insist on a search party to head out and look for her. Anna pressed her lips together. What would Ethan think of her if she got lost? He already had such a low opinion of her.

Anna shook her head. Why on earth did it matter what Ethan Wilder thought? She'd already determined that there was no pleasing the man, despite his apology. He was too set in his ways. Besides, he'd never find out that she'd been momentarily lost.

She smiled. That grouping of trees up ahead looked familiar. Hadn't she just passed them before she realized she might be lost? With a determined lift of her chin, she set off again. She'd be back to the cabins before anyone even realized she'd been gone.

Chapter Eight

"You're out of your mind, Nate. I can't take that woman all the way to Oregon."

Ethan glared at his younger brother. First Harley was putting thoughts in his head, and now Nathaniel was trying to do it, too.

"If she's dead set about going, you have to take her, Ethan. I made a promise to Cora last year."

"Your harebrained promises are of no concern to me." Ethan lifted a steaming tin mug of coffee to his lips.

The strong and bitter drink was a welcome change from the taste of mint in his mouth, but after the first couple of swallows, his mistake became evident. A sharp pain jabbed him in the gut. Clearly his stomach wasn't ready for anything other than the broth Anna had made and the willow bark tea. Cursing under his breath, he set the mug on the table. He raised his eyes to his brother.

"I ain't the right person to take Miss Porter to Oregon, or anywhere else, for that matter," he said, gritting his teeth when another painful jab poked his insides.

Nathaniel eyed him with his head cocked to the side. "Are you afraid of Anna Porter?" His eyes lingered on Ethan's hand over his stomach.

"That woman might finish me off for good if she comes near me again," Ethan grumbled.

His brother grinned like a fox in the henhouse. "I don't think she's got her mind set on putting you in an early grave, but that's not what I meant when I asked if you're afraid of her."

Ethan smirked. He wasn't going to add fuel to the fire by asking Nate to explain his question.

Nathaniel raised his own mug of coffee to his lips. "I'd never ask it of you, Ethan, but with Cora being with child, I'm not willing to put her through a journey she doesn't need to make, and I can't be gone that long if I were to go alone. I can't go back on my word to Anna that I'd get her to Oregon this summer." He paused, then slowly said, "I suppose I could ask Trevor and Travis."

Ethan lifted his eyes to his brother. "I wouldn't trust anyone with those two. They're both still wet behind the ears, especially Travis. He don't listen to anyone or lets anyone tell him what to do."

"I remember Pa saying the same thing about you."

Ethan clenched his jaw. He stiffened, making his already-sore stomach muscles hurt.

"Then you oughta know that trusting the safety and well-being of anyone to Travis would end badly," he growled. He stared at Nathaniel, curbing the urge to punch his brother for yet another reminder about his past failures. Hadn't he been tormented enough in the last day with thoughts of how he'd failed his parents?

Nathaniel watched him with a smirk on his face and a challenge in his eyes. Ethan ran his fingers through his hair. He'd been backed into a corner.

"I can't travel with a woman," he said. "How's that going to look to other folks? She wouldn't like her reputation sullied like that. An unmarried lady don't travel with a man."

The door squeaked on its hinges, and Harley walked in. The old man stopped in his tracks, glancing from Nathaniel to Ethan. His mustache and beard shifted when he smiled.

"Who's an unmarried lady?" he asked.

"Anna Porter," Nathaniel said quickly before Ethan could tell Harley it was none of his concern.

"Are ye thinkin' o' weddin' up with her, Ethan?" Harley's eyes sparkled with hope. Ethan ground his teeth.

"We were discussing how I'm going to uphold my promise and get Anna to Oregon," Nathaniel explained with a wide grin on his face.

"There ain't nothin' ta discuss." Harley stepped fully into the cabin, his eyes on Ethan. Harley reached for the mug Ethan had set on the table, sniffed it, then topped it off with hot coffee from the pot by the hearth.

"Ethan's the only choice ta do it," Harley said after taking a long slurp.

Ethan shook his head as his frustration grew with his brother, Harley, and even his own thoughts swirling in his head. The day before, he'd briefly entertained the idea that he should be the one to escort Miss Porter, especially after his dream about his mother. After his attempt at making amends with her over his behavior the last couple of days, the thought had vanished as quickly as Anna had rushed from the cabin.

"I ain't going to Oregon, and especially not with a woman in tow," he growled with a note of finality, more to get the thought out of his head than for his brother's or Harley's benefit.

He stepped around Harley and yanked the cabin door open. The fresh air felt good on his face. His eyes roamed the yard, traveling to the barns and lingering on the cabin Anna shared with the two younger Hudson sisters. Patrick sat along the creek with a fishing pole in his hand.

Movement from Nathaniel's cabin caught his eye. He groaned inwardly as the woman who seemed to be the bane of his existence the last couple of days emerged. Ethan took a small step back to conceal himself in the shadow of the cabin. She glanced his way, but didn't appear to see him. She seemed undecided about something, then, instead of heading his way, she walked behind the cabin toward the trees.

Ethan's eyes followed her until she disappeared into the woods. A satchel hung from her arms. He shrugged. Maybe she was going to collect some plants. He inhaled a deep breath, then headed back into the cabin and braced for another onslaught from his brother and Harley. Sure enough, he'd barely closed the door when the old man came at him.

"Ya could wed up with her, then there'd be no cause fer Anna ta leave." Harley took a long drink from the coffee mug.

"Leave me be, old man. I'm saying it for the last time. I ain't weddin' up with anyone." Ethan moved toward his bunk. The smell of coffee lingering in the air made his stomach twist into knots. There wasn't any of Anna's broth left that had soothed him earlier, so he reached for some of the mint Aimee Osborne had given him.

"You could pretend to be her brother if you take her to Oregon," Nathaniel offered. "No one would question it. Cora thinks of Anna as a sister, which makes her family to me and you already."

Ethan shook his head. He nearly laughed at the absurdity of Nathaniel's suggestion. While the thought of Anna as his wife was ridiculous, thinking of her as a sister was even more unfathomable. He turned his back to his brother and frowned. No. Whatever thoughts might have ever crossed his mind about Anna Porter, none of them had come close to anything brotherly.

* * * * *

The door to the cabin creaked. Ethan lifted his head from his bunk, catching a glimpse of a skirt between the gap in the curtain and the ground. He sat upright and swung his legs over the mattress. He blinked away the dizziness when he stood. Had Anna returned? His stomach growled. He could sure use some more of the broth she'd made the day before. It was all the nourishment he'd been able to keep down.

"Is anyone in here?"

Ethan frowned. It wasn't Anna. The voice belonged to Caroline. He slipped an old cotton shirt over his head that he'd dug out of his trunk earlier. It didn't have any buttons, only strings at the wide opening at the neck. He stepped into his boots, then pushed the curtain aside The dull throb in his hand worsened. The girl stared at him when he stepped into the main room.

"I'm looking for Anna," Caroline said, her eyes on his bandaged hand.

"She ain't here." Ethan glanced around the room to prove his point.

"She told Cora earlier that she was going to help me fix supper. I haven't been able to find her, and no one else has seen her since she left Cora's cabin several hours ago."

Ethan wrinkled his forehead. He'd seen Anna walk into the woods earlier. Had that been several hours ago?

"Where's Trevor or Travis?"

"I don't know. They rode off earlier this morning and haven't been back. I was about to find Nathaniel and ask him if he would look for Anna, but Patrick told me he and Harley went off to check on their traps. They took Josie with them. They said they weren't going to be gone long, but I'm getting worried."

Ethan's eyes fell on his rifle propped by the door. "I think I know where she might have gone off to. I saw her earlier." He frowned at his own words. If she'd been gone for hours, she might have gotten lost. "I'll find her," he added.

"You will?" Caroline's surprised wide-eyed look was almost laughable. "I mean, are you sure? Your hand won't give you trouble?"

"I don't need my hand to walk." Ethan moved to the door. He grabbed for a water skin and powder horn that hung on the wall and draped them around his neck and shoulder before reaching for his rifle.

"Tell Harley and Nathaniel I've gone looking for Anna, due north of here. I'll bring her back."

Ethan left the cabin without a backward glance at Caroline. He shook his head to dispel the lingering dizziness. It was time he got back on his feet. No more dawdling around the cabin, getting weaker by the hour. It had been nearly forty-eight hours since he'd drunk that vile tea that made him sicker than a dog. A good walk in the woods would perk him up quicker than lying around in bed all day.

Picking up Anna's footprints in the soft soil was no problem. It appeared as if she'd gone for a leisurely stroll, stopping every once in a while to, presumably, look at her surroundings. She didn't seem to have a clear destination. Her tracks led through the forest, following the easiest and most accessible path possible, around downed logs and dense shrubs. What had prompted her to head into the woods alone?

He must have covered a good mile when her footfalls became less noticeable where the ground turned rocky. Ethan focused on spotting broken twigs or scrapes on rocks made by her shoes. He reached a small clearing when it became evident that she'd realized that she was lost. She'd turned in a circle, then backtracked a short distance, then gone in a completely different direction.

Ethan shook his head. Fool woman. Why would she go somewhere unfamiliar, especially if she hadn't told anyone which direction she was heading? The sooner she left the valley, the better. He scoffed. Nathaniel's conversation came back to him as he continued to follow Anna Porter's tracks. If she continued on her present course, she would come to a dead end, unless she planned to climb some steep rocks.

He glanced up at the darkening sky. It wasn't so late in the day that he'd run out of daylight if he didn't find Anna soon, but the grey clouds moving in from the west meant he might get wet.

"Wouldn't be the first time Miss Porter is the cause for me getting soaked," he grumbled out loud.

A slight breeze tickled the back of his neck, lifting strands of his hair that grew nearly to his shoulder. A shiver passed through him. What if she was hurt? Not only did she have to navigate dead trees and dense undergrowth in this area, but the terrain was getting steeper, and sharp rocks or hidden boulders could cause anyone to slip and fall.

"Blast it woman, where are you going?" he called into the breeze. His answer was the faint trickle of water as it splashed across rocks.

She had to realize she wasn't anywhere close to where she'd started her walk. Either she was deliberately going in this direction, or she was hopelessly lost and disoriented. No doubt it was the latter. At least he hadn't seen any indication by the tracks she'd left that she might be injured.

Ethan stumbled over a large rock that had been concealed by dense undergrowth. His rifle saved him at the last second from falling, using it as a crutch to keep him on his feet. His left hand was completely useless at the moment. He cursed under his breath. He was still weak. His hand throbbed painfully and his stomach rumbled from lack of food. He lengthened his strides with the thought of Anna lost and probably scared. Just one fall and she could break her leg, or worse.

The spring cut through the rocks further ahead, tumbling over boulders on its way down the slope and into the valley several miles away, where it would meet up with the creek that flowed through Harley's Hole.

"If she's got any sense at all, she'll follow the stream," he mumbled. A smile cracked his face when her footprints indicated she was doing exactly that. Maybe she wasn't as helpless as he'd thought after all. Perhaps she'd realized that if she followed the water, it would take her back to the valley.

His path along the creek was quickly blocked by the thick growth of berry bushes that grew along the water's edge. The terrain here sloped downhill and became rather steep in spots, the uneven ground concealed by shrubs and undergrowth. Crossing the creek would make for easier footing on the other side.

Ethan studied Anna's tracks. They stopped at the water's edge. He scanned the rocks closer to the creek. There was a mark on some of the slime in the water that indicated that she might have attempted to cross here.

"You should have gone further upstream where it's safer and not as steep and slippery," Ethan said under his breath.

He stepped into the water, choosing his way over the slick rocks and staying clear of the thorny bushes that grew over the edge of the creek. Many of the branches dangled in the water. The stream wasn't deep, reaching midway up his calves, but the bottom was slippery with scum and uneven rocks.

Ethan gripped his rifle in his right hand as he set one foot in front of the other. His sole made contact with a sharp rock that moved as he stepped on it. He swayed slightly to keep his balance while at the same time, the sound of breaking twigs alerted him to something behind him.

"Mr. Wilder?" a woman's voice called.

Ethan's head turned. His foot shifted and twisted at the ankle when the slippery rock moved under his weight. Water splashed his face as he went down, the creek's current carrying him several yards downstream. His arm snagged in some overhanging branches, the sharp, long thorns tearing his shirt and scraping his skin. Ethan cursed, while Anna Porter frantically called his name. Thunder rumbled somewhere in the distance.

"Mr. Wilder, are you all right?" Anna called again. She stood as close to the water's edge as possible without getting snagged by the thick brambles, reaching her hand out to him.

"Stay back, woman, or you'll hurt yourself." Ethan glared at her while he yanked his shirt free of the barbs. One of the needle-sharp thorns sliced the skin of his upper arm. He hissed. More sharp pain seared his injured hand as the water penetrated through the bandage.

Carefully, he scrambled to his feet among the slick rocks. He held back a curse when pain shot up his leg when he put full weight on his right foot. Anna leaned forward, reaching for him.

"Are you all right?" Wide eyes stared up at him, moving from his face to his right arm. "You're bleeding."

Ethan glanced at his arm and torn shirt. Traces of red discolored the tan cotton. The puncture made by the sharp thorn throbbed, as did the injury to his hand, but what stung worse was that he'd had the mishap in the first place, and in front of Anna Porter, no less.

He eased the weight off his right leg, using the rifle to balance. He'd never been this accident-prone in his life. Had he been with his brothers, they'd have been mocking him mercilessly. There was only genuine concern in Anna's eyes.

"What are you doing here, Mr. Wilder?" she stammered.

Thunder rumbled again, this time much closer. Anna shrank back, staring up at the sky.

He glared at her. "I've been asking myself the same question. You're going to be the death of me, woman," Ethan grumbled as the first drops of rain began to fall.

Chapter Nine

Anna stared up at Ethan. Water soaked his shirt and britches, and the glare in his eyes was reminiscent of a couple of days ago when he'd stood before her in a similar fashion. At least this time, there was no mud on his face, and she wasn't the one responsible for him getting wet.

Or maybe it was her fault again? He'd slipped right after she'd called out his name in surprise. Although relief had swept through her at seeing someone familiar, the last person she'd expected to see in the woods while she'd tried to navigate her way back to the cabins had been Ethan Wilder.

"What are you doing here, Mr. Wilder? Shouldn't you be resting?"

Ethan's muscles along his jaw tightened and he clamped his lips shut. Clearly, he had something he wanted to say but kept it to himself. His chest heaved, then he spoke.

"Caroline was worried about you since you were gone for several hours without telling anyone where you went, so I came looking to make sure you weren't lost." His words sounded like a predatory growl.

Anna swallowed. Truth be told, she had been lost. Walking off into the woods on her own had been a foolish thing to do, but she wasn't about to concede that fact to this man.

She'd made her way through the forest, hoping to see something recognizable when she'd come upon the creek. She'd been sure that if she followed it, she'd get back to the valley. The problem was, she'd needed to find a way around the dense brambles. She'd tried to ford the creek, but the slippery rocks had made her reconsider that option. Ethan's fall had clearly proven she'd made the right choice.

"And you believe me incapable of finding my way back?" she challenged.

He smirked. "You're about three miles from the cabins. Don't tell me you weren't lost."

Anna straightened. "At least I managed to remain on my feet. I may have been lost, but I believe this creek would have led me back to the valley."

His silent glare was her answer that she'd been correct. He moved around her, hissing under his breath when he stepped on his right foot. The drizzle falling from the sky grew steadily stronger. Anna swiped at the moisture on her face.

"I'm sorry, Mr. Wilder," she said, following him as he hobbled away from the creek. "That remark was uncalled for. I appreciate that you've come looking for me."

He stopped, tossing a quick glance at her over his shoulder. "We'd best hurry back or you're going to be as soaked as I am."

He lurched forward, limping in the opposite direction from what she'd presumed was the way to get home. Anna caught up to him, glancing at the tear in his shirt near his shoulder. The fabric was stained red and blood still oozed from a wound no doubt made by one of those bushes with the sharp thorns that lined the creek.

"I don't think you're in any condition to travel fast," she said. "I can handle a little rain."

He continued forward, his knuckles white as he gripped his rifle in his right hand, staring straight ahead. Navigating up the rocky incline, he led her back the way she'd come earlier. Clearly, he seemed to know exactly where he was going. With each step he took, his limp became more pronounced. His damp shirt clung to his shoulders, making the rigid muscles of his back and shoulders visible. Ethan was clearly in a lot of pain, but too stubborn to admit it.

Once the ground leveled out, he stopped and pulled his water skin from around his neck and fumbled to uncork the opening. He took a long drink, then held it out to her. She started to shake her head to decline, then thought better of it.

Anna stepped closer, taking the pouch from him. Instead of drinking, she corked it to save him from trying to do it himself with only one usable hand.

Stubborn man.

She studied his face as he stared down at her. It was difficult to tell if all the moisture on his forehead was from the rain, or if he was sweating. Concealed pain glistened in his eyes.

Thunder rumbled through the mountains, and the rain came down in thicker drops.

"Can we find some shelter?" Anna asked, lifting her shawl over her head. She'd endure the walk back to the cabin in the rain if she had to, but pretending to want shelter might be a good way to get Ethan to slow down. His pale face was worrisome, but he would never admit to needing her help.

"A little further, the rocks can offer some shelter. There are some boulders that hang over a small outcropping."

Anna smiled eagerly, letting him lead the way again. By the time they reached the place he'd mentioned, her shawl was soaked. After ducking under the natural roof, a shiver passed through her and she rubbed her hands up and down her arms.

"Perhaps the rain won't last long," she suggested.

Ethan looked at her, still standing in the rain. He glanced at her, then at the ground at her feet. There was plenty of room for two people to comfortably take shelter, and it was dry.

"I'll get a fire started. You look cold." He set his rifle on the ground, then moved to collect wood that hadn't gotten wet. Anna gathered leaves and pine needles for tinder, making a small pile at her feet. Wordlessly, Ethan sat on the ground and pulled a piece of flint from one of the pouches around his neck. Barely able to hold it with his bandaged hand, he struck the flint with his hunting knife, creating a spark.

Anna added wood as a flame erupted on the leaves. She settled on the ground near the fire, hugging her arms around her waist. Ethan stared into the flames, his face as hard as ever. His jaw tightened when he adjusted his leg. No doubt he regretted that he'd come looking for her.

Would she ever do anything right in this man's eyes? Not that it mattered. She'd be gone from Harley's Hole soon, and then Ethan Wilder would become a distant memory. Her walk had given her plenty of time to think about how she was going to get to Fort Hall. If Nathaniel could get her at least that far, she'd do whatever was necessary to continue on with a group of settlers heading west, even if that meant marrying someone in need of a wife. If Cora's husband wouldn't take her, perhaps Harley or even the twins could be persuaded to go.

Ethan added more wood to the crackling fire. Anna's eyes fell to his arm and the wound that continued to bleed slightly.

"I have some salve in my satchel that I was supposed to give to Trevor for your hand," she said tentatively. "Aimee Osborne left it behind. I could put some on that cut. It looks painful."

Her eyes met Ethan's when he looked at her. His expression was unreadable, although the hard planes of his face had softened compared to the way he'd glared at her earlier by the creek. Surely, his male pride was wounded for having fallen into the water in front of her. Her remark about it hadn't been helpful to lighten his mood, but darn it, the man had deserved it.

Ethan glanced at his arm, lifting and flexing it. No doubt the deep stab from a thorn had torn into his muscle and hurt more than he was letting on.

"I might as well take a look while we wait for the rain to stop," Anna coaxed.

Waiting for you to get over your stubbornness might take forever.

She offered a smile when the lines along his forehead deepened. Finally, he nodded, but he did so while frowning.

"How about the hand? That bandage looks like it got a good soaking." Anna pointed at the injured hand in his lap.

"It's fine," he mumbled.

She reached for his hand, lifting it, but paused when he resisted. His eyes flashed a warning, which quickly dissolved into something closer to what she'd seen the other day when he'd apologized.

"You don't need to fret over me, Miss Porter," he said. "If you want to look at the arm, I'm gonna have to take off the shirt. I hope that don't bother you."

Anna swallowed. She dropped his hand and quickly shook her head. She cleared her throat.

"Why would it bother me?" Her pulse raced, the same reaction she'd had to seeing Ethan without a shirt on the other day.

He looked at her, his eyes searching, then he actually grinned. Anna stared. She couldn't tear her eyes away even if she'd wanted to. His features transformed instantly from the hard, unfeeling brute he'd tried to portray to a ruggedly handsome man with kind eyes and so much hidden emotion.

He broke the spell by raising both arms and pulling his shirt off over his head. Anna blinked, still holding onto the glimpse of the man she'd just seen. A man Ethan kept well hidden behind his dark façade.

Her eyes widened at what he didn't hide. Unable to look away, her gaze pored over his torso until Ethan had completely removed the shirt. The orange glow from the fire played off the well-defined muscles of his arms and along his shoulders. The heat in her cheeks matched the flames that flickered and danced in front of her.

"Miss Porter?"

Ethan's brows rose with an expectant look. He'd already lowered his hands, holding his shirt in his lap. Anna shook her head, silently chiding herself for acting like a silly adolescent girl sneaking a peek at the boys when they went swimming in the creek back home in Ohio, as if she didn't know what a man in the nude looked like.

Yes, but you've never been this close to a man without his clothes on before.

At least not a conscious man. She'd seen Nathaniel last summer, after he'd been shot, but she'd hardly had the time or the inclination to look at Cora's husband while he hovered near death.

Thank goodness Ethan's wound was on his arm, rather than his thigh. Anna's face scalded some more with the images conjured up by that thought.

"Let me find the salve," she said, her voice cracking. She turned her back to him, reaching for her satchel.

Her hand trembled as her fingers fumbled inside her sewing bag for the tin of salve. She pulled out several swatches of fabric to see if any of them might be of some use to her, and a few folded handkerchiefs she'd meant to embroider. One of them might be big enough to wrap around Ethan's arm as a bandage to cover the wound.

Anna opened the tin. A strong medicinal odor wafted from the ointment, and she turned up her nose. Hesitating, she dabbed her finger in it before lifting her eyes to Ethan's face. He sat next to her, his upper body slightly turned away. He shot a quick glance over his shoulder.

"That stuff smells nasty," he said. "I sure hope it really is something for wounds. I must be out of my mind to let you put that stuff on me."

Anna raised her chin to look at him. "It's what Cora told me."

Taking one of the pieces of cloth, she dabbed at the blood that had begun to dry around the gash in Ethan's upper arm. He sat stiffly, his muscles hard and taut beneath her ministration. She hesitated, then touched her finger to his arm, applying the salve around the wound. His skin was warm, despite the chill in the air and the fact that he'd recently tumbled into the cold water.

Her focus drifted from the wound to the rest of his upper body. Several more cuts and scrapes, presumably from his altercation with the thorny bush by the creek, crisscrossed his back and shoulders. Wordlessly, he raised his arm away from his torso while she wrapped a handkerchief around his bicep, covering the wound.

"You have cuts all over," she said quietly. Her finger reached out to touch one of them on his upper back. Ethan flinched slightly. Anna jerked her hand away. Her fingers trembled and her mouth had gone dry.

"Does it sting?" she asked.

"No," he murmured, which sounded closer to a growl.

Anna adjusted her position behind him to get closer. She owed him her gratitude for coming to look for her. If he had stayed at home, he wouldn't have added these additional injuries to his growing list.

She dabbed more ointment on the larger cuts. Ethan's rock-hard muscles seemed to melt beneath her touch, encouraging her to continue. The tips of her fingers slid along his skin, applying the healing salve to even the tiniest of scrapes.

The tingling feeling grew stronger the longer she made contact with him, rushing through her fingers and up her arms. Her breathing slowed while her heart began to pound faster. Anna jerked her hand back when a loud crack of thunder made her flinch.

"I think that's all of them," she whispered.

Ethan didn't move, except for his chest expanding when he drew in a breath. He fumbled with his damp shirt to pull it back over his head. He shifted his position next to her to where his back was no longer turned.

"Perhaps you should allow your shirt to dry by the fire for a while," she suggested, avoiding eye contact. She cringed at her inappropriate words. She dared a quick glance at his face. A faint smile formed on his lips. To hide her embarrassment for making such a bold suggestion, Anna responded with a smile of her own.

"I'll be fine, but thanks for doctoring me up."

"It's the least I could do. I'm sorry that, because of me, you're in more pain." Anna glanced at his hand.

"Make me some more of that broth you gave me yesterday, and we'll call it even."

She nodded. Their eyes met. The transformation in his features was astounding when he softened his stare and had that boyish smile on his face. Cora had told her that Ethan had once been a lot like Travis, and for the first time, she could almost believe it. His hesitant smile held a hint of his younger brother's mischievous attitude.

Ethan shifted again, setting his injured hand in the dirt for support. He instantly flinched and cursed under his breath. Anna's hand reached out to steady his arm.

"I keep forgetting about that damn hand," he growled. The softness in his features vanished again.

"Mr. Wilder, please let me see to your hand," Anna pleaded. "Your bandage is wet. That can't be good for the wound."

His frown was back, but he seemed to agree, holding out his hand for her to remove the thick bandage Aimee Osborne had applied.

"I believe I have enough cloth to wrap your hand again, and it should hold at least until we get back to the cabin. Your brother or Caroline can apply a better bandage."

The wound looked clean. Hopefully there would be no lasting damage from such a cut. Anna carefully applied some of the ointment around the stitches, the tips of her fingers gliding over his calloused palm. The warmth and weight of his large hand in her lap sent her heart beating faster again.

"I'm afraid I'm not very good at this." She glanced up at him, smiling uneasily as heat crept up into her cheeks. As quick as she could, she wrapped a clean piece of cloth around his hand.

Her heart must have skipped a beat as her eyes met his. He was looking at her, his gaze more intense than anything she'd seen before. It was almost a predatory stare, but nothing that would cause her to be afraid, at least not in a way that would make her fear he might harm her. Quite the opposite. There was no anger in his eyes, no contempt, yet something just as strong drawing her in.

"Seems to me you're doing just fine," Ethan said, his voice low and almost sensual.

Anna fought to move a breath of air past the constriction in her throat. She blinked and pulled her eyes away from his, then scooted back and away from Ethan. Their faces had been so close, much too close.

She fumbled to return all the items she'd taken out back into her satchel. She had to direct her focus elsewhere. Ethan's stare was simply too unsettling. At this moment, it would be better if he yelled at her and called her witless. Too many tumultuous feelings and sensations coursed through her, and none of them made any sense.

"Looks like the rain has stopped," she said, looking out beyond their natural shelter. "We can be on our way back to the cabins. No doubt everyone is worried about where we are."

She scrambled to her feet, brushing twigs and leaves from her skirt. Ethan struggled to stand, leaning heavily on his rifle for support. He still favored his right leg.

"Are you well enough to walk?" Anna asked tentatively. She should have offered to look at his ankle, but a sudden need to get back to the cabins rushed through her. This entire encounter with Ethan Wilder was too unsettling and confusing.

"I'll be fine." He kicked dirt onto the fire to put it out, then stepped up to her. "Once my hand is healed, I'll take you as far as Fort Hall, Miss Porter," he said, then limped off into the forest.

Chapter Ten

"You're absolutely sure this is what you want to do? You can still change your mind."

"Yes. I have to do this." Anna glanced up from folding the last of her dresses and packing it in the traveling trunk. Looking into Cora's hopeful eyes, she offered a weak smile to her friend, who stood a few paces away, holding several folded blankets. Anna stood and held out her hands to take the items. "We've been over this so many times."

"I know, but it doesn't hurt to ask again."

The loud banging of a fist on the cabin door saved Anna from offering a response. It was bad enough that she'd had second thoughts about leaving everyone she considered family behind and heading off into the unknown. Something inside her told her it was the right thing to do, that she would find out who she truly was if she made this journey. Here in this wilderness valley she would never fill the emptiness and loneliness in her heart.

"Come in," Cora called. The door swung open as if a strong blast of wind had pushed it, sending in a cloud of dust. Travis and Trevor stood under the frame. Travis moved first to step into the room.

"Ethan's acting like the entire day's wasted already, and the sun hasn't even been up more than an hour. He's asking if everything's ready to go." He grinned at Anna. "You sure you want him to take you to Fort Hall? Trevor and I can be ready to leave in five minutes."

"This is the last of my things." Anna placed the blankets in the trunk and closed it. She smiled at Travis. "Thank you for your offer, but I think I'll be all right." She pointed at the trunk. "You can take this to the wagon. Please let Ethan know I'll be ready to leave in a moment."

The twins each lifted an end of the trunk and disappeared out the door, Travis mumbling something under his breath. Anna smiled and shook her head. While the two brothers might be more entertaining company on her way to Fort Hall, Ethan was, no doubt, more trustworthy. Not that Travis and Trevor weren't experienced men in their environment, but their youth made them impulsive, especially Travis.

Everyone had been surprised three weeks ago when she and Ethan had returned from the woods and he'd announced that he would take her to Fort Hall. He'd used the excuse that someone needed to go for supplies, so he might as well take Anna along. Harley had simply chuckled and smiled gleefully, while Travis had complained that it was his turn to go to the supply depot this summer.

Ethan had been silent for most of the walk out of the forest that day, and Anna hadn't pressed him to speak. He'd clearly been in pain the way he'd favored his right leg, which probably hadn't done much to improve his mood. She'd had her own thoughts to contend with at the time. Her nearly intimate encounter with Ethan Wilder under the rocky overhang had been much too unsettling.

Everyone had seen her return from the forest with him. Back in Ohio, gossip would have brought her morals into question for being alone with a man in the woods. Here, no one cared, although Josie had looked at her with a worried expression on her face. Anna had smiled at the girl to assure her that everything was all right. Harley had looked rather pleased about something.

"Are you absolutely sure that you want to be the one to take me to Fort Hall?" Anna had asked Ethan before they'd parted ways that day.

"I said I would take you, or would you rather Travis and Trevor escort you?" Ethan had looked at her with raised brows, a challenge in his eyes. To her great surprise, there had even been a faint hint of a smile on his face.

Anna had stared back at him, still unable to fathom the change in his appearance. Without his constant scowl, he was a surprisingly handsome man.

"I just don't want you to regret your decision, Mr. Wilder." She'd raised her chin. She'd seen a different side of Ethan Wilder that day than the man he liked to portray to everyone else, and it gave her courage to challenge him. "Like you said, I might be detrimental to your health. You may not live to tell about your adventure."

He'd stared back for several silent seconds, his eyes sharp and focused on her face, as if he couldn't comprehend her light-hearted remark. Those eyes had darkened the longer he looked at her, not in anger, but in the same way he'd looked at her when she'd administered the salve on his hand. An inexplicable shiver of pleasure had run down Anna's spine, leaving her even more unsettled and her mind reeling with thoughts she didn't understand. Nathaniel and Harley had reached them at that moment, breaking their eye contact.

"You might be right, Miss Porter," Ethan had said in a low tone. "Guess I'll just have to keep my wits about me."

"Wits?" Travis had sauntered their way, glancing suspiciously from his oldest brother to Anna. "Didn't know you had any."

Ethan's scowl had returned as he'd glared at his brother.

"You'd best see to his hand, Trevor," Anna had quickly interjected, before the brothers' exchange erupted into a full verbal spat. "It may need a better bandage." She wouldn't mention the wounds he'd sustained because of his mishap in the creek in front of everyone. It would have simply raised questions Ethan surely didn't want to answer, especially with his brothers in attendance.

"You gave us a scare, Anna," Cora had said. "Caroline came to find me after Ethan set out to look for you. When it started to rain, I almost sent Nathaniel out to look for both of you. Why didn't you tell us where you were going?"

Anna had shrugged. "I needed some time to myself. I suppose I got lost. I have Ethan to thank for finding me." She'd smiled at Cora. Her gaze had darted to Ethan for a second and her heart sped up when he'd looked at her. Had that penetrating stare always been there and it was something she'd simply become aware of after what had happened earlier, or was it new? Anna had forced her eyes to Cora again.

"I'd best change out of these clothes. They're still damp after the rain." She hadn't looked back as she'd excused herself and scurried to her cabin.

Cora's assessment that Ethan was not the kind of man he tried to portray to everyone had become more evident that day. A man who didn't feel anything or care about anyone wouldn't have come looking for her when he'd thought she'd been lost, especially when he was still recuperating from his near-poisoning. Clearly, something about his past haunted him enough that he preferred to keep a cold demeanor, even with his family.

He'd returned to his sullen quietness as soon as they'd returned to the cabins. For the next three weeks, he'd been polite whenever they'd crossed paths when everyone took their meals together, or during the few occasions when they'd happened to be in the main cabin at the same time.

She'd caught him looking at her from across the yard a few times, but he'd rarely sought her out to talk to her except to discuss details about the upcoming journey. The day after they'd returned from the woods he'd let her know again that he wasn't going back on his word and would take her to Fort Hall. He'd anticipated his hand would take a couple weeks to heal, and if they planned to leave in three weeks, there would be wagon trains arriving at Fort Hall by then, so the timing would be in her favor. Cora had offered her the wagon and her team of mules.

"I can't accept the wagon," Anna had quickly declined.

Cora had taken her hand and stared at her in a way that left no room for argument. "You will take the wagon. I have no use for it anymore. And we don't need the mules, either. Besides, how else are you going to get to Oregon? Your chances of being accepted by one of the wagon outfits will be much greater if they see you have a good rig and team to pull it. At the very least, you might be able to sell them in exchange for passage."

Anna's attempt to decline again had been met with a firm finger raised to silence her.

"All right. Perhaps Ethan can bring it back," she'd mumbled. Arguing with Cora was pointless when she was that set about something. Having a wagon for the journey to Fort Hall had eased her worries of how she would manage to ride a horse the entire time. She'd driven the wagon much of the time last year, and she'd drive it all the way to Oregon if she had to.

After Cora's announcement that Anna would be taking the rig, Ethan, along with Nathaniel and the twins, had made any necessary repairs to the wagon and gotten it ready for travel.

"Well, I suppose it's time to go." Cora sighed next to her in the cabin while Anna still gazed around the small room she'd shared with Caroline and Josie for the last six months. Her pulse increased and she wrung her sweaty palms in front of her. She blinked and mentally shook her head. She had to do this, but would she be as nervous about leaving if Nathaniel escorted her rather than Ethan?

She glanced at her bed in the cabin one last time. It was time to go. She drew in a deep breath and blinked away the sting in her eyes. Her decision not to stay in this wilderness had been made ever since she'd first arrived here last year, and she wasn't going to back out now.

Ever since her encounter with Ethan in the woods, her need to leave had grown even stronger. She'd spent too much time over the course of the last three weeks thinking about him and her confusing reaction to him. She'd felt the stirrings of attraction, no matter how many times she'd tried to deny it.

They shared nothing in common. The thought of Ethan courting anyone, let alone her was almost laughable. He may have a soft heart buried somewhere inside, but he seemed too set in his ways to let go of his unapproachable demeanor. Besides, how could she have eyes for a man who was so unlike the only man she'd ever loved? No doubt Ethan hadn't even given their encounter a second thought.

Reaching for her shawl on the bed, Anna followed Trevor and Travis out the door. They stowed her trunk in the back of the wagon, which had already been packed with the rest of her meager belongings. There would be a lot of room in the wagon this time as compared to when she had traveled with Cora and her sisters and Patrick. Even though Cora had packed a few provisions to get her to Fort Hall, she'd have to buy more for the journey to Oregon, but she'd still be traveling light.

Caroline and Josie stood by the wagon, somber looks on their faces. Patrick ran to her and nearly threw his arms around her. He stopped at the last second and glanced over his shoulder to the twins. Apparently, he'd been listening to their nonsense about how men couldn't display emotion. Perhaps they'd all allowed Ethan to fill their heads with the idea that a man had to remain distant and unfeeling.

"Come here, Patrick." Anna grabbed the boy and wrapped her arms around him, leaning over slightly. She no longer had to kneel to be at eye level with him. He'd grown so much in just one year, and a rush of sadness swept through her that she wouldn't see him grow into a man. He stood stiffly for a second, then threw his own arms around her neck. The strong odor of fish and dirt came from his shirt.

"Don't leave, Anna," he whispered against her shoulder, sniffling.

"I have to, Patrick. Someday, maybe you can come and visit me when you're a little older." She broke away from him, smiling at the boy she'd known since his birth. She held back the tears that stung her eyes.

Patrick nodded. He hung his head and stepped away from her. Anna reached her hand out to Harley, who cleared his throat and pulled her into an embrace of his own.

"Gonna miss havin' ya here, Anna. Shore aint' gonna be ta same without ya an' yore biscuits." He leaned back and smiled, then winked at her. "Ya keep that Ethan in line, will ya? He may be ornery like a bear with a burr in his pelt, but he don't mean it. An' don't let 'im tell ya otherwise."

"I'm sure Ethan and I will get along fine." Anna smiled at the old man. He pulled a handkerchief out the top of his shirt and made a big show of blowing his nose.

"Darn'd spring flowers. They make my eyes 'n nose itch," he grumbled.

Anna looked to the twins. She shook each of their hands, meeting their gazes. For once, Travis didn't have any teasing words to offer.

"Keep learning about healing people, Trevor. You're good at it. And, you, Travis, take more responsibility around here. You're a good man, and I know everyone can trust you with their lives. Prove it to them."

He stared at her, then nodded wordlessly.

Caroline stood off to the side with Josie, dabbing at her eyes with a piece of cloth.

"I know you'll be a wonderful doctor someday," Anna whispered, embracing the younger girl who had been like a sister to her all her life. "Follow Aimee Osborne's advice and go to medical college, and don't let anyone tell you it's impossible."

Caroline nodded against her shoulder, her body shaking with sobs. "I'll miss you so much."

"I'll miss you, too." Anna peeled away from her, swiping at her eyes. Forcing a smile, she faced Josie.

"Look at all you've accomplished since we left Ohio," Anna said to the youngest Hudson sister. Quiet and meek Josie, who now wore britches and could shoot a rifle as well as the men, looked at her with a somber expression. She didn't cry. She'd done enough of that in her young life. "You're the strongest person I know."

"I'll come visit you in Oregon someday," Josie said when they embraced. "I'm heartbroken that you're leaving, but I understand it's something you have to do."

"Thank you," Anna whispered. She smiled and gave Josie a final squeeze.

Nathaniel pulled her into a brotherly embrace when she reached the front of the wagon.

"Wish you'd stay. I have you to thank for bringing Cora and me together. You were the only one she'd listen to when we first met."

Anna smiled at him. "I think your charm's what finally won her over. I had nothing to do with that."

101

Anna glanced at her best friend. Cora flung her arms around her after Nathaniel let her go. Her body as well as Cora's shook as they clung to each other, sobbing.

"Take good care of yourself, and it won't be too long before your baby arrives. You'll be too busy to even think about me."

"It won't be the same without you," Cora rasped. For once, she seemed at a loss for more words.

"You found your destiny here." Anna glanced from her to Nathaniel. "I can't even imagine you anywhere else."

"I hope you find what you're looking for. I'll get a letter to you somehow after the baby is born."

"I'd like that."

Anna gave her one final hug, then raised her foot to the wagon wheel to climb up into the driver's box. She swiped her hand across her face and inhaled deeply. Her eyes drifted to Ethan, who sat on his horse several yards away, watching.

Her heart sped up. This was really happening. She was leaving, and with the most unlikely of men she could have chosen to lead her to Fort Hall. Anna unwrapped the reins from the brake handle, and gave Ethan a nod to let him know she was ready. Ethan's horse moved toward her, coming up beside the wagon.

"You sure you can drive the team?"

She raised her chin, ignoring the wild beating of her heart at Ethan's perusal of her. His eyes drifted from her hands holding the reins to her face.

"A little late to be asking me that, isn't it?"

Perhaps she was mistaken, but it looked as if Ethan grinned just before he reined his horse away from her and rode past the mules to lead the way out of the valley. Travis yelled something to him, and Ethan raised his hand without a backward glance.

Anna clucked to the team, slapped the reins against their backs, and the wagon lurched forward. She didn't look back when several people called to her to have a safe journey. Her vision blurred and she blinked away the tears.

She was doing the right thing. She'd been strong enough to leave everything behind when she'd left her broken heart in Ohio. She could do it again. For now, all she had to do was follow the man who rode his horse a good fifty yards ahead of her.

Chapter Eleven

Ethan reined his horse to a stop along a meandering creek, his eyes scanning into the distance. An eagle screeched overhead, soaring toward the glowing ball of fire sinking lower into the horizon to the west. A soft breeze drifted over the grassland, making the tall blades sway back and forth as if in a dance. The leaves of the cottonwoods that lined the water rustled loudly, while behind him, the jingle of harnesses and the squeaking of wagon wheels drew closer. He inhaled a deep breath.

What on earth had he been thinking?

That question had grabbed hold of him for the last week like a wolverine sinking its deadly fangs into its prey.

Ethan shifted in the saddle. He glanced over his shoulder even though he didn't have to look to know that she'd catch up soon enough. Anna had driven the wagon every day since leaving the valley with no complaints, keeping up with the pace he'd set. If he'd been alone, he could have covered the distance much faster, but with a wagon, it meant moving at a crawl. By tomorrow, they'd finally reach their destination.

He lifted his hat from his head and raked his hand through his hair. Why had he impulsively told Anna that he'd take her to Fort Hall?

You know why, you fool.

He'd known Anna Porter for months, yet this had been the first time he'd really taken notice of her as more than one of the women his brother had brought to the valley. So, he'd done the first thing that had come to mind to put some distance between them – he'd offered to take her to Fort Hall. No matter how often he'd called himself crazy for his rash decision, he couldn't have gone back on his word.

Later, he'd reasoned that someone needed to go to Fort Hall for supplies anyway, so he might as well take Miss Porter along and deliver her there. She'd wanted to leave the valley, and it was for her own good. Unfortunately, he didn't believe his own excuses. He wanted her gone for different reasons. Reasons he hadn't wanted to think about at the time, and still didn't want to think about now. Trouble was, his mind wouldn't give him any peace.

Since that day when she'd gotten lost in the woods, he'd needed to put as much distance between himself and her as possible, if he wanted to keep his sanity. Once she was out of his sight for good, his life could get back to the way it had been, without his mind wandering into territory he'd sworn he'd never cross.

He hadn't been able to get Anna out of his thoughts. Getting gutted by a moose couldn't have produced a more powerful jolt of emotion. Since then, he'd spent more time lying awake at night than was healthy, remembering those soft fingers on his skin, or her warm, tender eyes looking at him.

Stupid fool that he was, that day she'd gotten lost he'd brazenly tried to make her nervous by removing his shirt in front of her. He'd noticed how it had made her uneasy to see him bare-chested once before, and he'd needed to get the upper hand after his embarrassing mishap in the creek.

His plan had backfired on him in the worst way possible. He hadn't counted on her feminine touch and the way it had soothed his battered and heated skin. Her soft and gentle hands on him while she'd doctored his scrapes and bruises had been sweet torture – for him.

She'd stirred a part of him he'd thought had died alongside his folks and little sister, and she'd done it without even realizing it. The way her fingers had moved as they'd applied the salve to his wounds had almost been seductive and purposeful, but he knew her better than that. Her actions had been completely innocent, yet they had ignited a fire in him that he hadn't been able to put out. And he'd decided right then and there that she had to go. She was becoming too dangerous for the kind of life he'd made for himself.

Ethan shook his head to try to rid himself of the images of her sitting so close to him under a rocky shelter. Her damp shawl had framed her soft face, while her skin and lips had glistened with moisture. Eyes, soft like a doe's, had stared back at him, cautious and confused. She'd been taken off guard by their encounter as much as he. It had taken all his willpower not to find out what she'd do if he kissed her.

He rotated his shoulder to dispel the sudden tingling feeling on his skin, as if Anna's fingers caressed him at this very moment. The breeze did little to cool the heat coursing through him.

All these years since leaving his old life behind and following Harley into the wilderness, he'd made it clear that he liked to keep his distance from people. It was easier than forming attachments. His family called him surly and grumpy like an old bear, and that was fine by him. His reckless days, along with emotional attachments, had ended when his folks died. Someone had to step up and be responsible and sensible in the family. He'd fallen short before, and his parents had paid the ultimate price for it.

Anna had stood up to him when she'd accidentally tossed the water at him. Whatever had happened that day and all the mishaps that followed, it had awakened something dormant in him. He hadn't figured out whether it was the fact that she'd put him in his place for his foul mood, or for some other unexplainable reason.

For the past three weeks, most everyone had stayed out of his way, accusing him of being more cantankerous than ever, which had suited him just fine. At least when he kept folks at arm's length, he didn't have to get too close to anyone. Of course, Harley had nearly come undone with happiness when Ethan had told him he'd take Anna to Fort Hall.

"Ya doin' the right thing, Son," the old codger had said, slapping him on the back. His face had lit up as if he'd struck gold.

Nathaniel had taken the news with a suspicious look in his eyes and a smirk on his face. Ethan had dared him with a scowl to say what had been on his mind. Nathaniel was much too perceptive and looked as if he'd read his thoughts. His younger brother had wisely kept his mouth shut.

The last five days on the trail to Fort Hall had only made his troubles worse. She'd kept up with the fast pace he'd set without a single complaint. During their first night, he'd set up camp in silence, and she hadn't said much, either. She'd fixed a meal of biscuits and meat, which they'd eaten in awkward silence. She'd quickly excused herself, saying she was tired from the long day, and had disappeared inside the wagon. Ethan had sat by the fire long into the night, reminding himself why he had to keep his distance.

"Do you expect to get to Fort Hall within a week?" she'd asked the next morning after helping him break camp and get the mules hitched to the wagon. She'd climbed into the driver's seat, looking at him for an answer.

"If we push hard, it'll be about six or seven days. Depends on whether you can keep up."

Her brows had shot up at his comment. Ethan hadn't been able to suppress a smile, no matter how hard he'd tried to remain impassive. Something about Anna awakened the man he might have been, had the tragedy with his folks not occurred. His brothers had always found pleasure in trying to rile him for his moods. Anna's quiet personality and the way she'd calmly dressed him down on several occasions for his demeanor was appealing.

"I think I can manage to keep up with you, Mr. Wilder." Her eyes had flashed in a haughty challenge.

Although she'd always been rather reserved and sensible, he'd seen that playful side in her a few times with the other women and with Patrick. He'd never paid much attention to it before. Like the day in the woods, it was different out here on the trail, when it was only the two of them and he was completely focused on her.

"Then let's not waste any more time," he'd said with a nod and reined his horse away from the wagon. The harnesses had creaked and jingled behind him as he'd led the way in the direction of Fort Hall and getting Anna Porter out of his life.

"What a beautiful spot," Anna called from behind him. Ethan shifted in the saddle to glance over his shoulder. She'd nearly caught up to him. "Is this where we're making camp for tonight, or do you plan on going further?"

He nodded toward the sun sinking in the horizon. "Best to stop here. There's water and good grass for the animals."

There was a hint of relief in her eyes and a faint smile on her lips as she pushed some loose strands of her dark hair back under her bonnet. Gritting his teeth, Ethan pulled his gaze away from her and nudged his horse toward the water. There was a sheltered spot to make camp for the night under the cottonwoods.

Ethan dismounted once his horse reached the creek and dipped its head to the water. He flexed his left hand, bringing feeling into his fingers. The wound had healed nicely, but there was still a lingering lack of sensation where a large scar ran across his palm. His sprained foot had taken less time to heal. Trevor had suggested he not wander in the woods for a while. Travis had chimed in that he should spend more time with Anna Porter, that if they were lucky, she might finish him off for them. Ethan had silently agreed with his brother.

He hobbled his horse, then moved to the wagon to unhitch the mules. After a long day, they were eager to get to water and grass. Anna climbed down from the driver's box. Her foot stepped on her skirt as she descended and she nearly lost her balance. Ethan rushed to her side, but she recovered before he reached her. She turned her head to him, surprise registering in her eyes.

"Guess I'm a bit clumsy from sitting in the jostling wagon all day," she said with a faint smile. She adjusted her bonnet on her head and rubbed her hand across her forehead. "If you'll start a fire, I'll get supper ready."

This had been their routine since the first night. While he tended to the animals, she prepared supper. They'd sit at the campfire, mostly in silence or making meaningless small talk. She'd been as reluctant as he to speak of anything that involved personal matters.

"If you'd like, Miss Porter, I can try and rustle up a rabbit or something for supper," he offered once a nice-sized flame crackled in the small pit he'd created.

"That would be nice." She offered a smile, glancing over her shoulder, then continued to rummage in the back of the wagon for her Dutch oven and the coffee pot.

A strong gust of wind whipped her skirt around her legs, and her bonnet blew off her head. Ethan stepped closer and reached for the handle of the heavy cast iron pot to lighten her load. She fumbled with the bonnet that hung from its ties around her neck and flapped at her shoulder, then raised her eyes to his with a grateful look on her face. Ethan swallowed past the sudden dryness in his throat.

"Don't you think it's time you called me Anna?" she offered with a hint of shyness in her voice.

Ethan cleared his throat. "I s'pose you should have called me by my first name a long time ago. You don't call any of my brothers by their surname."

He peeled his eyes away from her and took a step back. He stood much too close to her, letting him notice every little detail about her face. The freckles on her nose, the way the setting sun played in her eyes, the slight quiver of her lips.

Damn! His hand formed a fist at his side to keep from reaching out and touching the smooth skin of her cheek. Ethan gritted his teeth. He set the Dutch oven near the fire, then abruptly stomped off to pull his rifle from his saddle scabbard. Without looking back, he followed the creek, putting some much-needed distance between himself and Anna.

By the time he returned with a pair of jackrabbits that populated the tall grasses along the creek, Anna had a pot of coffee sitting in the coals next to the flames. The aroma drifted on the breeze before he reached camp. She stood with her back to him, leaning over the fire as she stirred something in her oven that sat next to the pot. With the sun going down, she must have decided to abandon the bonnet. Her dark hair hung down her back in a long braid.

The strong breeze nearly blew his hat from his head, the wind having shifted and gusting from behind him. As he reached up to secure it, the hair along the nape of his neck raised and an inexplicable feeling of foreboding rushed through him.

His eyes went to the woman by the fire. He rushed forward, dropping the rabbits and his rifle. Anna's skirt, which had blown toward the flames, had caught fire.

110

"Anna," Ethan roared.

She spun on her heels to stare at him, then looked down. The shock of seeing her clothes on fire clearly sent her into a panic. She screamed as she ran.

"Don't run," Ethan called. She didn't listen. He caught her around the waist as she fled toward the wagon, and pushed her to the ground, landing on top of her to smother the flames. He rolled with her in the dirt until the flames were out.

His chest heaved and his heart pounded like a stampede of elk when he twisted to the side and off of her. The last time fear had gripped him with such force had been the day he'd returned to his parents' camp, seeing all the smoke from the fire that had been set to the wagon and the lifeless image of his mother on the ground.

"Are you all right?" he rasped, forcing air into his lungs. He gripped Anna's arm, who lay on the ground beneath him, staring up at him with wide and fearful eyes. She nodded vigorously.

"Are you burned?" He shifted to look down her body at her legs. The skirt was tattered and charred in places, and would be useless. The petticoat underneath it looked singed, but not burned through.

"I don't think so," she said in a weak and cracking voice. She breathed as hard as he, her chest moving up and down in quick succession.

Ethan pushed away from her and stood, then offered his hand. She clasped his wrist as he pulled her to her feet with more force than necessary. The momentum brought her much too close. Anna's trembling hands braced against his chest.

"It's all right. You're safe," he murmured. His hand came up to push loose strands of hair from her face. This was not how he'd envisioned caressing her face, but he

111

couldn't have stopped himself anymore than stopping the wind from blowing.

"I know better than to run," she whispered. "I must have taken leave of my senses."

"It's a natural reaction," he offered. Her eyes shimmered as she stared up at him and her lips quivered in a thankful smile.

"Anna," Ethan uttered, and all his good intentions and willpower faded away in that moment.

Instead of releasing her, he held on and stepped closer. He bent forward, then his head dipped slightly. He hesitated. His hand fully cupped her cheek, his calloused thumb scraping across the softness of her skin. Anna's chest heaved against his as her body swayed closer.

The granite rocks he'd built around himself crumbled and crashed like a mighty waterfall that had been frozen in winter, and cracked with the spring thaw. His lips brushed hers in a light touch that couldn't be described as a kiss. It wasn't enough. He increased the contact, holding her steady as his fingers weaved into her hair at the back of her head. Rather than pulling away and telling him to stop, Anna leaned in closer.

Ethan abruptly pulled away. What the hell was he doing?

"I'm sorry," he growled through gritted teeth.

Eyes wide with surprise and confusion stared up at him. What on earth had come over him? He should be checking her for burns, not taking advantage of her.

Giving in to his impulse and kissing Anna had been the worst thing he could have done. Every moment he spent in her company, his resolve crumbled more. He couldn't surrender to the feelings she stirred in him. He wouldn't be able to endure it if he openly grew to care for her, and then lost her. What if he hadn't come back from his hunt when he had? She could have died. That thought sent a shiver of fear down his spine.

"It's getting late, Anna. Best take a look at your legs to make sure there are no burns before it gets too dark and change your clothes."

With those words, he strode off into the dim evening light beyond the fire to let the darkness surround him again.

Chapter Twelve

Anna pushed the Dutch oven out of the fire using some sturdy sticks. She carefully lifted the lid by slipping another stick under the handle and raising it. The delicious sweet smell of cobbler drifted on the breeze, mixing with the aroma of meat roasting over the spit and making her mouth water. It was difficult to see in the darkness, but the rabbits appeared to be cooked. If they remained over the fire any longer, they'd be charred.

She'd found some berries growing along the creek when she'd gone to bring water to camp. Fixing a sweet dessert for supper to go with the rabbits had been an impulsive decision. Preparing the meal had kept her mind and hands busy as the sun disappeared completely into the horizon, creating a dark curtain around camp.

Cooking, sewing, and keeping occupied with other domestic chores had always been her way of distracting herself from the sorrow in her heart. This time, it kept her from crumbling in fear and confusion. Fear, because she'd nearly lost her life today, or at least had almost gotten badly burned. The fear had been quickly replaced by confusion about what had happened after her near-fatal mishap at the campfire.

She glanced up, looking into the darkness beyond the reach of the firelight. Where was Ethan? He'd saved her life. Her fingers touched her tingling lips. He'd kissed her. She laughed softly. She hadn't thought about much else in the last hour, no matter how hard she'd focused on her task of preparing supper. He'd certainly taken her mind away from the frightening prospect of burning to death.

Why had he left so abruptly? Ethan Wilder was a difficult man to figure out. He presented a cold and hard persona on the outside to anyone who didn't know him, yet there was a warm and lighthearted man inside that he kept well concealed. There had been genuine concern for her when he'd shouted her name. She'd heard him, but she'd run in a panic anyway. As if catching the skirt of her dress on fire hadn't been careless enough, she'd made an even bigger mistake when fear had made her run. Ethan had been full of tenderness rather than anger when he'd told her it was a common reaction. He'd almost looked at her with anguish in his eyes.

Cora had read him correctly from the beginning. There was a friendly, caring man locked up somewhere inside Ethan Wilder. He wanted to keep people away, so he'd built an unfeeling wall around himself and created the rigid man his brothers constantly teased him about.

Yet, why had he allowed her to see more and more glimpses of his other, softer side? It had started that day in the woods, or perhaps even before, when he'd offered the apology for his behavior toward her. Did she want to know the reasons?

In two days' time, they'd be parting ways. It was ridiculous thinking about a man she'd never see again, but it was becoming more difficult not to think about Ethan. They'd been alone together for an entire week. While he hadn't been talkative, he'd been polite whenever they stopped to rest for the day and in the evenings.

He never carried a conversation, but he answered all her questions about anything from the mountains to the journey to Fort Hall and how soon he'd expect to get there. All without any of his usual gruffness that he displayed when he was around his family. She'd been careful not to ask him any personal questions, even though she had

115

sometimes led the conversation to his twin brothers and their antics.

A few times he'd even shown a faint hint of a smile when talking about Trevor and Travis, and each time he did, it made him appear years younger and less hardened. Ethan clearly cared for his brothers, even though he didn't show it, especially when they were in each other's company.

Anna added more wood to keep the fire going. She rubbed at her arms, the night breeze in the air sending a shiver down her spine. Why had she allowed Ethan to kiss her? Why *had* he kissed her? Her sudden and unexpected infatuation with Ethan Wilder over the last several weeks had steadily overshadowed the sadness she'd kept bottled up in her heart. Guilt nagged at her for setting aside Franklin's memory in favor of thinking about another man.

Despite his perpetual grumpiness, he'd slowly taken over a spot in her heart that had known only emptiness since Franklin's death. She shook her head. Ethan Wilder was the last man she'd ever considered catching her attention. Why had he sparked her interest now, after all the months of being acquainted with him? Ever since the mishap with the dirty water and finding out from Cora about his background, she'd been drawn to him. He'd known sorrow and loss, and that bonded them somehow. At least that's what she told herself.

Mindful of the flames and the direction of the breeze, Anna lifted the long skewer off the fire and set the meat on a tin plate. She stood as far away from the fire as possible. She'd hastily changed into a different petticoat and dress after making sure she didn't have any burns on her legs. She'd have to assess the damage to the dress the next day in daylight. Perhaps there were parts of the material that could be salvaged and put to use for something else.

"The food's going to get cold if he doesn't come back soon," she mumbled, and wiped her hands on her apron.

Where had that perplexing man gone? Apparently, the kiss had been as unexpected for him as it had been for her. Had he taken pleasure in it as much as she? Anna's cheeks heated at the thought. She had enjoyed Ethan's kiss, despite the fact that it had been uninvited. It hadn't lasted more than a second or two before he'd pulled away. That had obviously been enough time for him to reconsider his actions.

Holding a cool hand against her cheek, Anna shook her head. Nothing could come of this. She was heading west, and Ethan was returning to the mountains once he'd purchased supplies for his family. Besides, there was no reason to think that her infatuation was anything but one-sided.

Then why did he kiss you, Anna?

Something rustled in the grass beyond the light from the fire before Anna could explore the question further. She spun around. Ethan emerged from the darkness, his presence instantly making her heart speed up. What was she going to say to him?

"Supper's ready," she blurted. "You're back just in time before it gets cold."

"Smells good," came the deep voice.

Ethan stepped fully into the glow of the firelight, his eyes catching hers. Anna smiled for lack of something to say, then quickly dropped her gaze when he continued to stare.

"I'll get you a plate," she stammered. "Coffee's ready, too, if you'd like to pour a cup for yourself."

She turned her back to him and wiped her clammy palms against her apron, then dished up some cobbler and half of one of the rabbits. Ethan poured a cup of steaming coffee and leaned against the wagon's tailgate. He eyed the food on his plate when Anna walked up and handed it to him.

"I think Harley's right. We're sure going to miss your cooking," he said, stabbing a fork into the cobbler.

"I enjoy cooking," she answered in response to his . . . had that been a compliment coming from Ethan Wilder? Anna looked up at him to see if his remark had been a joke. He took another bite of the sweet cobbler, clearly enjoying it as he chewed.

"I hope it's all right," she added. "Most of the berries I found were ripe enough, but there might have been some that were still a bit tart. I think I added enough sugar to make it taste sweet."

His response was a nod and another bite of the cobbler. Anna lowered her head, suppressing a smile. She concentrated on her own plate while Ethan scraped his clean. Wordlessly, he moved to the fire and helped himself to another heaping portion of cobbler, then joined her again by the tailgate.

"Are your legs all right?" he asked between mouthfuls.

"Yes, I didn't get burned," she answered faster than she should have. The small talk was more awkward than on previous nights. "Thanks to you. If you hadn't been there, who knows what might have happened."

There was a silent pause, which seemed longer because his features were difficult to make out in the dim light. When he set his plate aside and shifted to face her, Anna strained her eyes to better see him.

"I want to apologize again for what happened earlier, Miss Por . . . Anna. I was out of line."

Anna shook her head. "I already told you, there is no need to apologize. You saved my life. If anyone was out of line, it was me."

"You?" His voice rose in clear surprise. The flicker of light from the campfire made the puzzled frown on his face look almost comical.

Anna straightened. She stared directly up at him. "I should have stopped you before you even had the chance to kiss me. I allowed it to happen. I simply wanted to –"

She stopped in mid-sentence. What had she wanted? Find out if she was ready to love again? She mentally shook her head. Not with a man like Ethan. He belonged in the wilderness, and she wasn't cut out for that kind of life. A year's worth of mourning and loneliness squeezed her chest. Ethan had taken all the heaviness away in that short kiss. He couldn't have missed the slight hitch in her voice. She blinked back the sudden tears in her eyes.

"I've only been kissed by one man before, my fiancé," she whispered because the tightness in her throat wouldn't let the words come freely.

Ethan lifted his hand to his head and raked his fingers through his hair. He murmured something under his breath that sounded like a curse word.

"Why aren't you married to him?" His question was more of a plea.

She hesitated, dropping eye contact. "He died." Her voice cracked. "He died and it was my fault." Anna turned away and sobbed into her hands. "I'm sorry. I shouldn't have let you –"

Ethan's leg shifted to take a step forward. He cut her off before she could finish. "Your fault? What happened?" He stood close enough behind her that his breath tickled her neck.

Anna swallowed to dislodge the growing squeezing of her throat. Taking in air became painful. "He had an accident because of me." She spun around, then took a step back when she nearly collided with Ethan. "Because I declined his offer to have supper with him, he's now dead."

Ethan shifted again. "That don't make any sense."

Anna scoffed. "Do you recall accusing me of always being so helpful the night your hand got injured . . . and when I nearly poisoned you?" She waited for an answer. When he simply nodded, she continued. "Franklin decided to continue plowing one of his fields into the evening since I'd told him I had to help Cora that night. He was working hard to get his farm ready so that we could get married." Scornfully, she added, "Because I helped out a friend, my fiancé died."

Ethan shook his head in obvious confusion.

"A neighbor found him later . . . dead under the plow." Anna sniffled. She wiped her hand across her eyes. "I was told he died instantly from a blow to the head."

That awful day played again in her mind when Mr. Jones, Franklin's neighbor, had come knocking on the door, letting her know that Franklin was dead. The sinking feeling of dread came over her, as if she was living through the ordeal all over again.

"I thought I could run away from my sorrow and guilt, so I told Cora I'd come with her and her family when she talked about heading to Oregon."

Ethan's body tensed, then he stepped up to her. His hand reached for her arm, hesitated, then pulled her toward him. Anna fell against his solid chest, accepting his surprising invitation to lean on him.

"Anna, what happened was an accident," he said slowly, his words rumbling in his chest.

She leaned her head against his shoulder, holding in the tears while he held her in his arms. It felt so good to be held by him, so unexpected and surprising. Crickets chirped all around them, drowning out her quiet sobs.

"But if I had been there with him, if I had accepted his offer to have supper with him that evening, he wouldn't have gone out in the field so late in the day, and it wouldn't have happened," she murmured into his shirt.

"Then it might have happened the next day, or the next, or several years from now. Accidents happen, and you can't blame yourself for something like that."

"But you blame yourself for what happened to your folks," she whispered, and instantly regretted blurting out the words. Ethan stiffened and dropped his arms from around her.

"That's completely different," he growled, the tenderness gone from his voice.

The fragile connection she'd made with him broke. He was clearly not ready to talk about his own past. Anna grasped his arm in an attempt to salvage what they'd started. She stared up into his dark eyes.

"I'm sure you understand about guilt, Ethan. Cora told me about what happened to your family, and how you feel responsible. I feel responsible for what happened to my fiancé."

"You didn't part ways with him in anger the way I did with my folks." Ethan's words were strained. "There was nothing you could have done to help if you had been there."

"I could have kept him from working that day," Anna tried to reason.

"My folks died because I wasn't there to help protect the family. Had I not insisted on going off on my own, defying my father, they wouldn't have set up camp along the river, and wouldn't have crossed paths with the men who robbed and killed them."

Anna shook her head. "You don't know that for sure."

Ethan turned away from her. His hand raked through his hair as he stared at the ground. "A part of me died with them that day," he murmured. Anna strained her ears to hear him.

"A part of me died with Franklin," she whispered, and stepped up to him. "But it didn't keep me from shutting out the people who still care about me."

There was a long pause. "I failed my family."

"Is that why you're so closed off to everyone? Because you're afraid you might fail them again?"

She reached her hand up to touch his shoulder. His muscles remained rigid beneath her touch. Her understanding of Ethan deepened. The strain in his voice was a clear indication that he'd never talked to anyone about his turmoil before. Neither had she, but her sorrow hadn't lasted as long as his. Anna's heart warmed as he'd exposed his vulnerable side.

Ethan's neck and jaw looked harder than stone. His shoulders tightened even more.

"You don't know anything about it," he said, the tone of his voice low and deadly calm, belying his rigid posture.

The flames from the campfire blazed in his eyes as he turned his head to look at her standing next to him. He pulled away from her and kicked at some dirt on the ground. He stepped around her, staring at the fire. Before she could say she was sorry for her words, he spun on his heels to look her way again.

"I'll make sure the horses are secured and I'll kill the fire. Best get some rest, Anna. Tomorrow we'll be at Fort Hall."

He moved toward the trees where he'd picketed the horses earlier. "Supper was good," he added as he walked away, leaving Anna to stare into the darkness.

Chapter Thirteen

Nothing about the white adobe structure in the distance had changed since the last time Ethan had been to Fort Hall several years ago. Hundreds of old army carts and equipment littered the countryside, decaying in the harsh elements. He or his brothers usually came later in the season to collect supplies for the winter, after most of the travelers heading west had moved through. This time, dozens of covered wagons camped along the creek that flowed past the old army outpost.

Ethan gripped his horse's reins tighter when an unexpected jolt ripped through his heart. With several wagon outfits here, it shouldn't be a problem to find a group who'd take Anna with them. He shifted in the saddle. Why did that thought bother him? This was the reason they were here – to send her off to Oregon.

His eyes scanned the distance while he honed in on the sounds of the wagon behind him. He reined his horse to a stop, waiting for Anna to catch up. Even though he should have offered to drive the rig, he'd ridden ahead for most of the morning to be alone with his thoughts.

He'd caught her rubbing at her arms on multiple occasions, but throughout the entire week she'd never complained that she was sore. The one time he had offered to drive the mules, she'd declined, and told him she needed to build her strength for the long trek to Oregon.

Ethan stared off into the distance, pushing his hat back on his head. He'd completely misjudged Anna Porter. For all the months he'd known her, he'd considered her too soft and weak-minded to live in this rugged environment, so unlike her friend, Cora.

He'd certainly changed his mind about her over the last month, and even more so in the last week. Anna wasn't weak, either in body or spirit. A slow smile spread across his face. He hadn't changed his mind that she was soft, however. In fact, he'd found out firsthand last night exactly how soft she was when he'd held her in his arms.

Ethan cursed under his breath. He rubbed at his tired eyes. He'd lain awake all night, thinking about the woman and how it had felt holding her, and making the mistake of kissing her. If thoughts of her tender touch on his bruised and battered skin hadn't been enough to torment him over the weeks, now he'd crossed the line into territory that might be impossible to get out of.

Then she'd had the gall to talk to him about his past. He'd never discussed with anyone how his folks had died, or the guilt he kept bottled up inside. Anna was only partially right about him. He was afraid of getting hurt again like she'd said, but it was more than that. Fear of letting down the people he loved kept him from forming attachments, along with avoiding the pain of loss.

His father had told him that fateful day that he was old enough to take more responsibility for his actions, and Ethan hadn't listened. He'd simply dismissed his father's advice as the ramblings of someone who wanted to keep a tight hold on him.

"It's time you set aside your impulsive foolishness, Ethan, and take some responsibility, before someone gets hurt." His father's voice echoed in his mind.

"How are you going to get hurt if I go off hunting?" Ethan had retorted. "For weeks, we've done nothing but travel, and I'm getting weary of riding along next to the wagon, or looking after my brothers. As you've said, I'm old enough. I'm going hunting, while you look after your children instead of having me do it. I ain't their pa."

His father had shaken his head. "It's not me I worry about, Son, but you. Someday you'll understand, and you'll do right by the ones you love and think of them before yourself."

"I'm done listening to you. For once, I'm going to make up my own mind." Taking his horse, he'd stormed off.

Those had been his last words to his folks. The day his father predicted had come sooner than anyone could have foreseen. Ethan squeezed his hand around the reins. He'd done the sensible thing from that day on, but it had been too late. He'd learned his lesson, but at what cost? While his rigid ways had made his brothers see him in an unfavorable light, he'd always put responsibility first. Right now, the responsible thing was to get Anna safely on a wagon train to Oregon rather than letting the call of his heart tell him she was better off with him.

The team of mules pulled up alongside his horse, and Ethan turned his head to look at Anna sitting in her usual spot on the driver's seat. She leaned forward, resting her arms on her thighs. When the wagon came to a full stop, she straightened, and pushed her hand into her lower back.

She hadn't said much that morning about what had happened the night before, or about their conversation. She still mourned the man she would have married, and it was just as well. Knowing that made it easier to let her go.

"It looks busier than when I was here last year," Anna called with a hesitant smile, nudging her chin toward the outpost.

"This is the right time of year when folks stop to rest before continuing on. Either here or Fort Bridger."

Anna laughed. Ethan stared at her. Her face was radiant when she looked happy, the way she did now. A knot formed in his gut, twisting it almost painfully.

"We were supposed to go to Fort Bridger, but we got lost after we couldn't keep up with our outfit Cora insisted on following last year." Her smile faded, and she looked directly at him. "Cora wouldn't have met Nathaniel, and who knows if we would have made it all the way to Oregon."

"She did a foolish thing," Ethan grumbled.

"She did what she thought was right for her family," Anna defended. "Sometimes that requires taking risks."

Ethan kept his mouth shut. Experience had taught him differently. Time to steer away from bringing family into the discussion.

"How do you plan on getting to Oregon?" The question had nagged him for some time, yet he chided himself for even asking it. His job was to deliver her to Fort Hall, nothing more.

"I'm confident that someone will be willing to take me along. Like Cora said, I have the wagon and a good team of mules. That has to account for something."

"And what if it doesn't?"

Did he really hope that she'd ask him to take her back to Harley's Hole if she couldn't find an outfit that would let her join up with them?

"Last year, our biggest obstacle was that we were unmarried women." Anna raised her chin, but she didn't make eye contact. "If I have to marry someone in order to be allowed to go, then that's what I'll do. As long as it's someone who has the same goals as I do."

Ethan wiped a hand across his face. Would she really consider marrying a stranger when she still mourned her fiancé?

"And what are those?"

Anna glanced at him. She evaluated his face for a moment, as if she was looking for something before answering. "He should be someone who is ready to leave the past behind and wants to make a fresh start, work hard, and values family."

Well, that certainly excluded him on at least one count. The past would always be with him, and he didn't need or want a family beyond his brothers. The saddle leather creaked when he shifted his weight. He nudged his chin toward the horizon.

"There should be a place to camp along the creek. Once we're set up, we can look around and see who's there and willing to take you on."

Ethan kneed his horse forward, but not before he caught the distinct glimpse of disappointment in Anna's eyes.

* * * * *

Ethan led Anna among the many wagons camped along the creek. After securing their own spot, he'd picketed the mules and his horse, and promised a young boy a penny to keep an eye on the animals for him. Not knowing any of the other people who were encamped here, he didn't trust that the animals were safe without someone watching them, but he wasn't going to let Anna wander around alone, either. At least the boy could alert the people around him if someone came into this camp.

"We'll ask around about any of the outfits while we're at the trading post getting supplies. See if any of them suit you."

Ethan gripped his rifle, his eyes in constant motion as he surveyed his surroundings. It had been a while since he'd mingled with this many people. Women in various camps washed clothes by the creek or tended cooking fires, while men stood around talking and making repairs to their wagons.

Several people looked up from what they were doing to watch as he and Anna walked past them. Wide-eyed, her eyes darted around. She was definitely nervous. Perhaps she was having second thoughts about going to Oregon, now that she was here at the fort. Why did that thought lighten his chest? If she'd changed her mind, he'd break camp immediately and take her back to Harley's Hole.

Ethan stopped once they were past most of the camped wagons and before reaching the gate. The trading post was just beyond the walls.

"You still want to go through with this?" he asked, facing her.

Anna stared up at him in surprise. Or was that a hopeful look she tossed at him?

"Through with what? Of course I still want to go to Oregon. Where else would I go?" Her hands were clasped tightly in front of her, belying the confidence she tried to convey.

"You don't have to go to Oregon, Anna. You could have returned to Ohio." Where had that thought come from? Ethan kicked himself mentally, but it was too late to backtrack on his words. Ohio seemed safer for her than Oregon. At least she'd be somewhere that was familiar to her.

You could ask her to come back to Harley's Hole. You could keep her safe there.

No. He didn't want to keep her safe. He shook his head in frustration as his thoughts got in the way of each other. Yes, of course he wanted to keep her safe, but hadn't he concluded a long time ago that she was safer somewhere other than in the wilderness? Why, then, did he want to take her back to Harley's Hole?

Anna gave a short laugh. "I don't want to return to Ohio. There's nothing but memories for me there. Besides, there's no one heading east as far as I know."

"Joseph Walker was heading east. He was going all the way to Boston. You could have gone with him, but it's too late now. He left weeks ago."

Ethan looked up when two men started shouting and arguing a short distance away. Several Indians milled about, trying to peddle their wares to some of the emigrants outside the gate. When one approached, Ethan stared at him. Making eye contact with Ethan, the Indian clearly read the unspoken message to stay away, and he backed off. Ethan tensed. Anna didn't belong here among these people, or among a bunch of strangers heading west. Harley's Hole suddenly seemed like the safest place for her.

"I heard Joseph was heading to look for a girl who's presumed to be dead?" Anna's brows rose, looking up at him. Her forehead wrinkled.

Ethan refocused his attention on her and the conversation he'd started.

"I only heard part of the story from Harley and Daniel. They're always full of tales about the old days, as they call it, but apparently the girl's French father and Indian mother were killed, and a mutual friend took the little girl and escaped to Boston. Her Bannock grandfather thinks she's alive and Joseph promised to find out and bring her back to him".

"That's a long way to travel to find out if a child is still alive." Anna shook her head.

"She would be a grown woman now. Her folks died more than twenty years ago while fur trappers still sought their fortunes in the mountains."

"Well, I hope Joseph finds her, or finds out what happened to her." Anna took a step forward to head to the fort. Ethan followed, unable to delay talking to the trader any longer.

A man rushed past them from behind at that moment, bumping into Anna and nearly knocking her to the ground. Ethan's hand reached out to steady her. He tucked her behind him and faced the man, who was dressed in greasy buckskins that were tattered and worn. He stopped to stare. Anna flinched against Ethan. She let out a quiet gasp.

The older woodsman's face was unshaven and dirty, his fur cap drawn low over his head, like so many other men who frequented the trading post when they came out of the mountains. That wasn't what made him stand out, however. One of his eyes was covered with a leather eye patch, giving him a gruesome appearance. With his good eye, he stared at Anna, a slight leer on his face.

He bowed his head slightly and pulled his fur hat dramatically from his head, exposing matted hair that hung to his shoulders.

"Beggin' yore pardon, ma'am." His insolent smile exposed rotten teeth. There was nothing in his tone that indicated his apology was sincere. Ethan stepped fully in front of Anna and faced the man.

"Next time, watch where you're going," Ethan warned, gripping his rifle in one hand. He met the man's cold stare, as his one eye drifted to him, looking him over as if taking his measure. Ethan smirked and shot a quick look to the man's hand, which twitched near the hilt of his knife hanging from his belt.

The older man was typical of so many of the mountain men who frequented the trading post. Former fur trappers who hadn't left the mountains after the fur trade had died down more than a dozen years ago. Many had found a new purpose as scouts and hunters for the wagon trains that came through the territory, since they knew the trails, the terrain, and the Indians. This man was as rough and mean-looking as many of the men Ethan had met over the years.

"Meant no harm to yer missus," the woodsman said, then moved past Ethan without a backward glance. Ethan stared after him until he disappeared into one of the buildings inside the fort, then turned his attention back on Anna.

"Are you all right?" He reached up to touch her arm. His eyes ran up and down her dress, as if the contact with the trapper might have damaged her in some way, like the fire that had burned her dress the evening before.

Anna shook her head. She offered a smile that left Ethan with a pounding heart. He dropped his hand that was touching her and gripped his rifle tighter. The urge to protect her and keep her safe washed over him like a creek overflowing its banks. No. He couldn't allow his heart to take over his thinking. He wasn't ready to risk more heartache in his life.

"No harm done," she said. "I'm sure it was just an accident."

Ethan shot another glance in the direction the man had gone. "Yeah, I'm sure you're right," he said absently. "Let's go see about those supplies at the trading post and if Stan Moray, the trader, knows any of the men leading the wagons. You stand a better chance of a wagon master letting you come along if he sees that you're well-outfitted."

The thought of Anna leaving on her own made his stomach churn again, especially after the encounter with that woodsman. Who would look after her and protect her from men like that once she was on her way to Oregon? He worked the muscles in his jaw and mentally shook his head. It's what she wanted to do, and it was best this way. He'd already started to care for her more than he wanted to admit.

Stan Moray, the trader, was haggling with an emigrant about the price of flour when Ethan led Anna into the building. The bearded man looked up, his eyes widening when he recognized Ethan. His gaze moved from him to Anna, then he returned his attention to his customer.

Ethan glanced around the store. As usual, prices for goods were extraordinarily high. Moray would bleed as much money out of the unfortunate travelers as he possibly could. The emigrant finally slapped some coins on the crude table made from planks of wood laid over a couple of barrels, and stomped from the store with his sack of flour.

"Ethan Wilder," Moray called. "Ain't it a little early for ya to be here? Woulda thought ta see one a yore brothers rather than you." His eyes drifted to Anna. His beard twitched. "Seems to me yore brother Nate was in the company of a lady last season. Has old Harley got you boys hitched up now?"

Ethan scowled at the man. "The lady needs enough supplies to get her to Oregon, Moray. The usual staples and dry goods. And she's not paying a penny more than what you'd charge me or my family." He set his rifle on the counter and leaned forward to stare the trader in the eye.

"Sure, Ethan. A friend of yors is a friend o'mine an' gets my special prices. Gotta charge them emigrants more, ya know. Gotta make a livin' somehow."

Ethan didn't respond. Moray's prices for the goods he sold to the emigrants passing through Fort Hall was downright robbery, but it wasn't any of his business.

"Do you know anything about any of the outfits camped here?" Ethan glanced over his shoulder when a man walked into the store.

Moray shrugged. "Jes the usual types. Farmers lookin' fer a better life or missionaries eager ta spread the gospel.

Tired and sore o' bein' on the trail so long. Why ya askin'?"

"Miss Porter is looking to find someone who'll take her along to Oregon."

"Lost yore husband, did ya?" Moray looked at Anna. He rubbed at his bearded chin. "Seems like Nate had the same question fer me last summer. Ain't that odd?"

"That would have been my friend, Cora," Anna supplied. The trader's eyes widened. He pointed at her.

"That's right. That was her name." He glanced back at Ethan. "What's goin' on with you Wilder boys? Operatin' a business ta get women sent ta Oregon?" He laughed at his own joke.

"Get the supplies together, Moray. I'll be back first thing tomorrow to pick them up." Ethan reached for Anna's arm. "Let's get back to camp. Maybe we can talk to some of the outfits."

Anna stayed close to his side as he led her to the door. The man who had walked in moments before stepped aside. He eyed Ethan, then Anna, then said, "Excuse me, I couldn't help but overhear. If you're looking for a way to get to Oregon, my company would be glad to take on another wagon."

Ethan narrowed his eyes, taking the man's measure. He was dressed in dusty trousers held up by suspenders over a wool shirt. The ends of his pants were stuffed in well-worn boots. The man reached out his hand.

"Jeremy Howell. I'm the leader of our group of families heading to the Willamette Valley."

Ethan eyed the offered hand, then shook it. "Ethan Wilder."

"A pleasure, Mr. Wilder. We lost several wagons in a river mishap about a week ago, and, God rest their souls, six members of our group died, including our scout."

His eyes widened and he held up his hand, as if he was worried that he'd said the wrong thing. "But not to worry. I already hired on a couple of men who said they could scout for us. They're very familiar with the territory." He chuckled as if something was funny. "One of them may look a bit off-putting with his eye patch, but the other man assured me he was completely trustworthy." He glanced from Ethan to Anna. "Did I hear you say only you were looking to go to Oregon, Miss? If you're in need of a husband, my cousin is in need of a wife."

Ethan stepped forward before Anna could respond to the question. The mention of a man with an eye patch sent a rush of apprehension down his spine. The man who'd nearly knocked Anna over outside the fort immediately came to mind. If his intuition was correct, there was nothing trustworthy about that woodsman.

Jeremy Howell seemed much too trusting. Regardless, the mention of Anna needing a husband made the pulse throb in his ears as his body tensed. Ethan cursed silently for what he was about to do, but there was no other way around it if he was going to make sure that Anna was safe on her way to Oregon.

"My sister and I would be glad to join your outfit, Mr. Howell."

Behind him, Moray coughed loudly, and next to him, Anna gasped.

Chapter Fourteen

"Ethan, what are you doing?"

Anna hastened her steps to keep up with Ethan's long strides as he rushed out of the trader's store and toward the gate leading out of the fort's yard.

"Heading back to camp," he said without looking back.

Anna grabbed his arm to slow him down, but he didn't budge. She hung on, trying to keep pace with him. She glanced at his profile, and the taut muscles of his cheek and neck.

"I meant, what did you do at the trading post, telling Mr. Howell that I'm your sister?"

"I'm taking you all the way to Oregon. Pretending to be your brother saves your reputation." He still didn't look at her. Dodging several men on horseback, he continued out the gate toward their camp beyond the outpost's adobe walls.

"What? But why?"

Anna collided against his hard body when Ethan stopped abruptly. He turned to stare down at her. The darkness in his eyes softened, as did the rest of his features. He still didn't look happy, however.

"Because you need someone to look out for you, and you shouldn't have to marry a stranger just to get to Oregon."

"But, you can't go with me to Oregon . . . as my brother," she stammered.

Why would he make such an impulsive decision in the first place? Protecting her from an unwanted marriage couldn't be his reason. The Ethan Wilder he tried to portray to the rest of the world wouldn't care if she had to marry someone or not. Anna leaned forward, her eyes narrowed. Her heart beat wildly against her ribs, and it wasn't due to exertion from trying to keep up with him.

He glared at her. "Taking you to Oregon is the responsible thing to do."

Anna didn't back away from his dark stare. The small glimpse of desperation and longing in his eyes was enough to realize that Ethan was fighting a battle with himself. He still guarded his feelings too much to say what might really be on his mind.

"But what about taking supplies back to Harley's Hole?"

Ethan chuckled. "If I'm not back home in a couple of weeks, Travis and Trevor will come looking for me. I'll leave word at the trading post where I've gone."

"You don't want to go to Oregon. Why would you do that for me, Ethan?" Anna pressed. He seemed to have thought of everything, yet his decision had been made at the spur of the moment. "You should return to your family. Besides, you already said I was dangerous to your health."

Ethan continued to stare at her. Her eyes widened when a slow grin spread across his face. Her limbs went weak at the instant transformation to his features. This was the true face of the man she'd slowly grown to care for over the weeks, much more than she dare admit to him, at least until she had less conflicting responses from him. More and more, he'd behaved in some way or said something that had made her wonder about his feelings, yet he was either too closed-off or too stubborn to admit it.

"You may be dangerous, but if I can survive you, Miss Anna Porter, I can survive anything," he drawled slowly.

"Even a trip to Oregon?" she challenged.

"Yes, ma'am, even a trip to Oregon."

Anna curled her toes inside her shoes to stop the urge to step closer and touch his face. Her cheeks flushed and she couldn't hold back a slight smile.

"I can't figure you out, Ethan Wilder. Do you realize you may have to drop your gruff façade and be cordial?" she teased. "Folks on a wagon train are friendly for the most part, and come together like family. I learned that on the journey from Independence to Fort Laramie last year." She inhaled a breath for courage, then pressed on. "Someday everyone is going to see the man you truly are. You won't be able to hide behind the pretense of being a coldhearted oaf any longer."

Ethan's smile faded. "Don't be so sure about that, Anna."

He dropped eye contact and resumed heading in the direction of their camp, retreating once again behind his veil of ice. Anna fell in step beside him. Boldly, she hooked her hand through the crook of his arm. She smiled when he shot her a quick look of surprise.

She leaned toward him and whispered, "It's perfectly acceptable, since you're my brother."

Ethan's jaw muscle twitched when she laughed to cover up the turmoil racing through her. Teasing Ethan became easier all the time, and as much as he tried to conceal it, it was obvious in his smiles that he enjoyed it, too, to the point where he'd teased her on occasion.

Leaving Harley's Hole and pursuing something unknown in an unfamiliar land had been on her mind all winter. Running away from the memories and guilt of her past had become less and less important the closer she was to her goal, and the man walking beside her was the reason.

Coming to Fort Hall today had left her nerves a jumbled mess, and rather than looking forward to finally heading for Oregon, she was nervous and unsure about her decision. Ethan's kiss the night before had changed everything, at least for her. It was still too difficult to read whether he had feelings for her, or whether the kiss truly had been an impulsive accident.

You're not bold like Cora to come right out and say what's on your mind, Anna.

What if she mentioned it and he didn't feel the same? It would be humiliating to ask him if he could ever consider courting her. Every time she'd even approached a personal subject, he'd closed himself off. It was best not to back a bull into a corner.

Anna released his arm once they reached their camp. The young boy sat on a tree stump, whittling a piece of wood with a small knife. He jumped up when he saw Ethan.

"Thanks for taking good care of the horse and mules," Ethan told the boy, who nodded and eagerly accepted the penny from the man. He ran from camp, back to his wagon that stood with a group of other wagons a short distance away.

"You made a little boy feel important and very happy." Anna came up beside Ethan, smiling as the boy disappeared from view.

Ethan looked at her, then frowned. "I'm just glad he stayed in camp and did what I asked."

"I can start supper if you get a fire going," she said, the awkwardness back now that they'd returned to camp. "You can still change your mind, you know." She raised her head to gauge his reaction.

His forehead wrinkled in a deep frown. "I ain't changing my mind. At first light, I'll pick up your . . . our supplies from Moray and find out when Howell's outfit is leaving."

"You might find out this evening." Anna nudged with her chin toward a man and woman heading their way, skirting around a few other wagons.

The man was Jeremy Howell and next to him walked a whip-thin woman about his height. Blonde curls poked out from under her bonnet as she bounced along. Her hands and arms flailed through the air as if she was waving off a swarm of hornets. Even from a distance, it was evident that she chattered non-stop.

The woman glanced in their direction at that moment, and a wide, toothy smile formed on her lips. She hopped up and down like a little schoolgirl, and waved enthusiastically. She grabbed Mr. Howell's arm and rushed him along.

"You know her?" Ethan frowned, looking at Anna, then back to the woman.

"Never seen her before in my life." Smiling, Anna raised her hand to return the wave.

Long before the couple reached the camp, the woman called out to them in greeting while she continued to wave her hand in the air. Anna suppressed a laugh when Ethan groaned. There was no time for him to walk away, if that had been his intention. Jeremy Howell approached, the woman next to him squealing in delight. If he'd spoken, his words had been drowned out by the loud woman.

"You must be Anna Wilder. It is so nice to meet you. I'm Marybeth Howell," she screeched, opening up her arms. To be polite, Anna raised her own arms for a quick embrace.

"Jeremy, my husband, told me all about you and your brother," she continued. Her eyes darted to Ethan, and her smile widened. "And what a handsome man he is." She flicked her wrist at him, smiling broadly while appraising him from top to bottom. "You won't have any trouble at all finding a wife in Oregon, Mr. Wilder, but women might be scarce out west from what I hear."

She turned her attention back to Anna, who waited to greet her guest.

"It's a pleasure to meet you, too, Mrs. Howell. I'm so glad that your husband –"

"Call me Marybeth, Anna. No need for formalities. We're gonna be such good friends in no time. You must come to supper at our camp." She flicked her wrist in front of her face. "I make the best corn chowder. Everyone always raves about it. Of course, back in Virginia, when we had fresh corn, it was much better." Her eyes sparkled, darting from Anna to Ethan. "The rest of the families are anxious to meet you. When Jeremy told us we were going to have another wagon join us, we were delighted."

"That's very kind of you, Marybeth. Is there something you'd like –"

"Supper's cooking over the fires right now. I told Jeremy we needed to stop by and invite you before you fixed your own, didn't we Jeremy?" She turned to her husband, then back to Anna without waiting for a response. "I'm always aware when new folks arrive, and make sure to invite them their first night. To be neighborly, you know. Back in Virginia we always had dinner guests nearly four times a week. Say you'll join us. We're camped right over yonder." She pointed at a group of wagons that were within easy sight.

Anna stared at the woman, then glanced at Ethan. His face was impassive, but a warning flashed in his eyes and there was a slight shake of his head. He looked as sick as he'd appeared that evening after drinking the vile tea she'd given him.

"If you'll be kind enough to give us a few minutes at our wagon, we'll –"

"Lovely. I do hope you like corn chowder. People always say mine is delicious." Marybeth clasped Anna's hands between hers as if she was trying to squash a pesky fly. "We'll see you in a few minutes. "Come along, Jeremy."

Abruptly, she turned and reached for her husband's arm, dragging him out of camp.

Anna's hand went to her mouth. She snorted, then laughed.

"You go. I'll find some jerky in the wagon." Ethan turned away from her and headed for his horse.

Anna reached out and grabbed his arm before he had the chance to walk away. "Oh, no. This was your idea. I'm not going to meet the rest of the people with whom we'll be traveling and make an excuse why you're not with me." She smiled up into his scowling face.

"Are you ill?" He did look rather pale all of a sudden. "I promise, I didn't feed you any puke weed, but you look sick to your stomach."

"I'm starting to feel that way," he grumbled.

Anna held his arm. "I think it's time to meet the folks with whom you'll be traveling, Ethan." She laughed at the growing displeasure on Ethan's face. "You said you could survive anything if you could survive me, remember?"

"You're not like that woman," he grumbled. "Is it too late to change my mind about going?"

Anna paused. A rush of dread came over her and the lighthearted mood she was in disappeared. Was he serious? The slight twitch in the corner of his mouth and the twinkle in his eye gave her the answer she needed.

"You have every right to change your mind, Ethan," she whispered, then held her breath.

He shook his head. "For some reason, I must hold you in high regard, Anna *Wilder*. Being around you is either gonna make me stronger, or it'll kill me."

He nudged his chin in the direction the Howells had gone, a clear indication that he was ready to face Marybeth Howell again.

"Let me grab my shawl."

Anna rushed to the wagon, raising her hand to her chest. She trembled when she reached for her shawl. Ethan had called her Anna Wilder, and that he held her in high regard. It didn't mean anything. He'd said it as a joke since Marybeth had called her by that name, but it had a nice ring to it. She mentally shook her head. Could she go through with this charade of being Ethan's sister? Could he?

"We'd better go now, or I'm gonna get cold feet."

Anna sucked in a surprised breath. A slight thrill raced down her spine at Ethan's deep voice so close behind her. How had he approached so quietly? He took the shawl from her hand and draped it around her shoulders, his hands lingering for a moment too long.

Anna gripped the front of her shawl, and nodded. She reached for his arm, allowing him to lead her to the other camp. Nothing about this felt as if she was his sister. Ethan's mixed signals continued to be confusing and aggravating. The man probably wasn't sure himself what it was he wanted.

They passed several camps of travelers, most of them looking trail weary. Oxen and mules appeared skinny, eagerly feeding on the grasses growing along the creek. They still had a long journey ahead of them, with some of the most unforgiving land yet to cover, from what she remembered folks saying last summer. The hot desert was still ahead of them, as well as impossibly steep mountains further west. Anna gripped Ethan's arm tighter.

"Thank you, for all you've done for me and continue to do, Ethan." She glanced up at him as they walked.

His steps faltered for a moment as their eyes met. Whether he was about to say something or not was lost when Marybeth's shrill greeting pierced the air.

"I'm so glad you're here. Come and meet the rest of the families." Her arms spread wide as if she was going to embrace them both, but she stopped short and simply stood in front of them like an eagle hovering over prey. Her sharp eyes went from Anna to Ethan, then lingered on Anna's hand gripping Ethan's arm.

Marybeth moved aside, and with a sweeping motion of her hand led them among a group of families who stood or sat around several fires within the circle of their wagons. The men stood, waiting their turn to shake Ethan's hand while Jeremy Howell made the introductions. His wife pulled Anna away from Ethan and toward the women.

"That brother of yours sure is protective," Marybeth proclaimed. "Doesn't want to let you out of his sights, does he?" She laughed. "I don't think I've ever seen a brother look at his sister the way he looks at you. I declare, I think I'd swoon if my own husband looked at me that way."

Anna groped for the right words as her pulse throbbed in her ears. What was Marybeth talking about? "Ethan's a very intense man. He's always been rather –"

"Let me introduce you to the family," Marybeth interrupted. "We've all traveled from Virginia. They might be a bit tired from the journey. I'm usually so energetic, but lately I've been so exhausted around midday. I just can't understand why."

She rattled off the names of the women in front of her, along with their relationship to her and the men who stood with Ethan. Anna focused on the introductions, but her mind was on the things Marybeth had said a moment ago.

"That's Mildred Howell, my sister-in-law. She's married to Pastor Albert Howell, Jeremy's brother. His cousin, Ed, lost his wife in the river crossing a week back.

Poor man has three little girls, but Cousin Maude and Cousin Millicent are taking good care of them."

Millicent smiled and shook Anna's hand. Maude waddled toward her, holding one hand to her arched back, which made her pregnant stomach more obvious.

Marybeth paused for a breath. "Of course, Ed's going to be looking for a wife in Oregon." She smiled brightly at Anna. "If you've half a mind to wed up with someone, he's a good man. He'd make a fine husband, wouldn't he, Mildred?"

"Ed's a hard worker. In fact, he –"

"And these are my young'uns, Sally Mae and Henry." Marybeth pointed at two young children. The boy couldn't be older than Patrick, and the girl must be about four.

"I've been teaching Sally Mae how to bake the most incredible molasses cookies. She really is a brilliant girl for her a . . . take your thumb out of your mouth, Sally Mae. That's not how a young lady behaves." Marybeth bent to grab her daughter's hand and pulled it away from her face.

"Young'uns," she mumbled, smiling at Anna. "Do you like children?"

Anna opened her mouth to reply that she loved children, but Marybeth flicked her wrist before she could say a word. "Of course you do. What woman doesn't love children, am I right, Maude?"

Maude nodded rather than reply verbally. No doubt she'd learned a long time ago that answering with words would be futile in Marybeth's presence. Boisterous laughter came from where the men stood. Anna glanced to find Ethan. He appeared to be listening to Pastor Howell.

"We can always use another good man on the trail," the burly man proclaimed. He chuckled, a bright smile on his face when looking at Ethan. His eyes drifted to the group of women, picking out Anna. "If your sister is looking to wed up with someone, Cousin Ed just lost his wife." He shook his head. "Sad situation, God rest her soul."

"Anna isn't looking for a husband." Ethan's words were strong and firm.

He glared at the man named Ed, then looked her way. Their eyes met and Anna's heart did a little flip in her chest. Ethan looked at her with his dark eyes, as if silently telling her he was not letting her go.

The pastor chuckled. "I understand your protectiveness over your sister, Mr. Wilder. I'm the same way. We have to look out for our women, don't we? I assure you, Ed is a good man. Perhaps once you get to know him better, you'll give your blessing."

Ethan grunted and mumbled something unintelligible. He stepped away from the men, beckoning to Anna.

"Let's all eat, shall we?" Marybeth called, and the men eagerly dispersed.

Ethan walked up to her. "I prefer supper at our own camp," he murmured so only she could hear.

"These are nice people, Ethan." Anna offered a smile. "But I don't like this charade."

Ethan frowned. "I don't, either, but what was I gonna do?" His jaw muscles tensed, and he nodded toward Ed. "Do you want to marry that man? I'll head home if that's what you want."

Anna grasped for his hand, staring up into his eyes. "No, that's not what I want."

Chapter Fifteen

"Why don't you let that sister of yours walk with me a spell, Mr. Wilder? I promise I'll bring her back. I always walk when I can. They say it's good for preventing consumption. Back in Virginia, I would walk every day to my friend Vivian's farm, but the countryside was much prettier there."

Anna groaned quietly on the wagon seat. Ethan suppressed a chuckle. He drew back on the reins to bring the mules to a halt.

"She's welcome to walk, Mrs. Howell," he called to the woman, who waited several paces away from the wagon.

"You have no heart, Ethan Wilder," Anna hissed under her breath, shooting him a glaring look.

"I've been told that once or twice." He leaned forward, resting his elbows on the tops of his thighs, a smile on his face.

"Come along, Anna, before he changes his mind."

"I won't forgive you for this," Anna whispered and moved to climb from the wagon.

Ethan held out his hand to steady her as she stood. She met his eyes when he didn't let go right away.

"You're the one who told me I needed to be more agreeable with the folks." His smile widened.

Anna's chest heaved and fell. She offered him another annoyed glare once she stepped off the rig. Ethan caught her face changing to a forced smile before she headed for Marybeth Howell.

"I do say, Anna. That brother of yours sure doesn't let you out of his sights. Ever since we left Fort Hall he's practically been your shadow. Is he always like that? I was telling Jeremy that a woman ought to have more of a say in the things she can and can't do. I mean, I tell him all the time he needs to tend the young'uns more. Goodness knows, I do all the cooking and washing, and . . ."

Ethan shook his head and clucked to the mules. He slapped the reins against the tops of their backs, and the team leaned into the traces. The wagon lurched forward.

For more than a week, the small caravan of six wagons had rolled along the desolate prairie, following the winding Snake River the first three days and taking Ethan further away from his solitary mountains. Although the Howell clan and their relatives were nice enough folks, the more time he spent around them, the longing grew stronger for the wilds of the mountains with their green meadows and sparkling streams.

The smile froze on his face. Another thing that had steadily grown stronger was his yearning for the woman who now walked behind the wagon with her newfound . . . friend. In Anna's company, he hadn't felt more at peace since he'd been a boy. Slowly, day by day, with each mile they put behind them, Anna had chiseled away a little more of the granite around his heart until there was none left.

She hadn't brought up his past since that night when he'd kissed her, and she hadn't talked about her fiancé, either. For all outward appearances, they'd assumed the roles of devoted siblings. Anna mingled with the other families as if she belonged with them. For her sake, he'd been friendly with the men, something that would have made old Harley proud and his brothers drop their jaws.

What Anna thought of him was most important, however. She often sought him out with a pleased smile on her face, so she must be satisfied with his demeanor around the others. More often than not, he'd wondered about what would happen once they reached their destination. It was still months away, and each day became more difficult than the one before to pretend indifference where Anna was concerned.

His feelings for her were anything but brotherly, but there was nothing he could do about them. For her sake, he had to continue to act indifferently. His admiration for her grew steadily, and he couldn't remember why he'd ever considered her weak or had wanted her gone from Harley's Hole. She was tireless and resilient, and she had the patience of a saint to be able to put up with a woman like Marybeth Howell.

Ethan grinned as he played with the leather reins in his hands. He'd enjoyed testing Anna's patience earlier when he'd indulged Marybeth's request for Anna to walk with her. Clearly, she hadn't been too pleased about it.

Anna seemed to enjoy the company of the other ladies and mingling with people again. She smiled more than he'd ever seen her smile at Harley's Hole, or perhaps he hadn't paid as much attention there. Ethan had seen her spend time with the three little girls that belonged to Ed Howell. What if she decided to marry him?

No matter how hard he tried, Ethan couldn't find fault with the man. He seemed to fit all of Anna's requirements in a husband. He was looking to start a farm in Oregon, he was a family man, and he worked hard. There was nothing he could do to stop her if she decided that Ed was the kind of man she'd been looking for. He simply had to keep reminding himself why he didn't want attachments.

Ethan stared straight ahead, scanning the vastness of the desolate prairie that stretched out in all directions. To their right was the winding Snake River, flowing through a steep canyon that was impossible to access from where the trail led them.

The vegetation along the trail was sparse, and each day the animals showed more strain due to poor grazing. Fresh meat was also scarce, and the two scouts Jeremy Howell had hired came back empty-handed from a hunt more times than not. The few rabbits they brought back weren't enough to sustain the group for more than a meager meal.

One thing was for sure. Ethan didn't trust those two men and kept his eye on them whenever he could. They didn't mingle with the families and kept to themselves. He'd thought about going off hunting by himself to see if he'd have better luck, but reluctance to leave the wagons out of sight held him back.

The younger of the two, Anton, eyed the women with too much interest, and Ethan had interceded once when the scout had followed Millicent away from camp one evening. Ethan hadn't planned to cause trouble with the guides, so he'd walked up to the man and struck up a conversation with him until Millicent had returned to her family.

The one with the eye patch, Oliver Sabin, bothered him even more. The man kept a low profile, only spoke to Jeremy when he needed to, and was away from camp frequently. When he was nearby, he'd often glanced at Anna, and Ethan had even caught the man studying him with a satisfied sneer on his face as if he knew something Ethan didn't.

Jeremy Howell called a stop to the day's travel along a small trickle of water out in the open grasslands. A few sparse trees grew here and there, but there was little shelter from wind or the elements. Ethan unhitched the mules and led them, along with his horse, away from camp to forage.

Anna was heading his way when he returned to the wagon. Evidently, she'd made an escape from Marybeth Howell. A small child ran toward her, then stumbled and fell, and instantly let out a loud wail. Anna knelt to the ground and scooped the little girl into her arms. Ethan rushed toward them.

"Ethan, I need some water," Anna called, carrying the girl to the wagon. "She scraped her knee. I don't think it's serious."

The child, one of Ed Howell's daughters, clung to Anna's neck, her tears leaving streaks on her dusty cheeks.

"It's going to be all right," Anna cooed. "We'll get you all fixed up."

Ethan dropped the wagon's tailgate and Anna set the girl on it, pushing her dress up her leg to expose a scraped-up knee. He dipped a tin cup in the water barrel strapped to the side of the wagon and handed it to Anna. She offered a warm smile.

"How would you like a sweet treat for dessert tonight?" Anna asked enthusiastically, no doubt in an effort to distract the child from her sore leg. The little girl nodded. Anna dipped a cloth in the cup, then cleaned the blood from the girl's knee. Using a different cloth she wiped her dirty face, then kissed her forehead.

Ethan groaned silently, standing next to Anna as she comforted the little girl. Old memories played out in his head of his mother consoling his little sister after she'd fallen at one time in much the same way. The past suddenly became the future – a long, solitary future. Then Anna appeared, filling his heart with love and taking away the loneliness and the guilt from his mistakes.

"Heavens, what happened?"

Marybeth's distinct screech pierced the air, pulling him from his daydreams. Somewhere in the distance, a hawk answered. The annoying woman swooped into camp, her wide eyes darting from Ethan to Anna to the little girl. Ethan backed away when Marybeth pushed her way to the tailgate.

"Hattie fell and scraped her knee. It's all better, isn't it, Hattie?" Anna smiled at the girl.

"I say, that girl needs a ma. Maude is heavy with child and can't chase after Ed's young'uns all the time, and Millicent and I have our hands full looking after our own. Every child needs a mother. We certainly don't want people to be calling her names when we get to Oregon. Children can be so cruel to one another."

"I certainly don't mind watching the girls for a while during the day," Anna offered. "We've gotten to know each other already over the past week, haven't we, Hattie?" The little girl smiled and nodded.

No doubt Marybeth would suggest again that Anna marry Ed Howell. No sooner had Ethan thought it, when the woman voiced her opinion.

"Well, in that case, you really need to think about getting married, Anna. Ed needs a wife, and I've seen you talking to him."

Anna's eyes darted to Ethan. If he could, he'd sweep Anna into his arms and kiss her right in front of everyone, and let Marybeth Howell know in no uncertain terms exactly what he thought of her idea.

Anna laughed softly. "I don't think there's a need for –
"

"Anna, you need a husband. Your brother isn't going to take care of you all your life," Marybeth chastised and shot him a stern look. "Isn't that right, Mr. Wilder?"

"Anna can take care of herself," Ethan grumbled. But he'd always be there for her.

Marybeth's eyes widened. She blew air through her nose. "Well, in that case, she ought to get married, like I said. Do you want her to become an old maid?"

"Is everything all right here? Hattie?"

Ed Howell rushed toward them, saving Ethan from answering Marybeth's question. His worried eyes shot to Ethan, then to his cousin and Anna.

"She's all right, Mr. Howell," Anna assured him. "Just a little -"

"She was running around unattended," Marybeth interrupted. "Why, if Anna hadn't been there, she could have been killed. And look how she's taken to Anna." She shot her cousin a meaningful look.

Ed Howell pulled his hat from his head. "Thank you, Miss Wilder, for taking care of my girl."

"Of course. She's a good girl. I promised her some sweets after supper. I hope you don't mind."

"Mind? Of course he doesn't mind, do you Ed? Why, you really ought to -"

Ethan gritted his teeth. He stepped up next to Anna. Everyone in this outfit might put up with Marybeth Howell, but that didn't mean he had to.

"I'm sure Jeremy is getting hungry and wants his supper, Mrs. Howell." He stared at the thin woman, whose eyes went wide at his interruption. Her mouth gaped open, but he continued before she could interrupt again. "And I'm sure Pastor Howell's wife expects you and your kids at their wagon, Ed."

Ed Howell nodded, avoiding Ethan's stare.

"You can come back later for some dessert, Hattie," Anna said quickly, coming to Ethan's aid. "And you can bring your sisters, too." She lifted Hattie into her arms and handed the girl to her father. He smiled hesitantly.

"Thank you again," he said, and headed toward his own rig.

"Well, if that were me, I would -"

"Go and fix your husband his supper." Ethan finished for Marybeth. Next to him, Anna coughed, which sounded distinctly like a suppressed chuckle. She cleared her throat.

"I'd best get supper started, too. Don't you agree, Marybeth?"

"Why . . . yes. As I was about to say, time to fix something to eat for Jeremy and the children." She glared at Ethan. "I can tell when I'm not wanted. Not everyone seems to appreciate sound advice. I guess I will go back to my family. At least there I know they care about what I say, and enjoy my cooking. I could tell the other night that you must not know good corn chowder when you taste it, Mr. Wilder." With a final huff, she marched from camp.

"Glad she was in agreement to leave," Ethan grumbled. Anna's lips pressed together. She held her hand to her hip in silent disapproval, but she couldn't hold the pose for long. Her eyes shone with laughter and her hand flew to her mouth to suppress her sudden giggles. Ethan smiled back at her. He had to turn away or he would go through with what he'd planned to do a few minutes ago, and kiss her.

"I'll get your cooking fire started."

* * * * *

Ethan offered Anna a cup of steaming coffee when she walked into camp. She accepted it with a grateful nod and a smile.

Speaking softly, she said, "The girls are back at their wagon, all tucked in. I think they enjoyed the peach pie. Of course, Marybeth had to tell me about the wonderful peach pies she used to bake in Virginia."

The fire crackled loudly, casting shadows on the canvas of the wagon. The camp had quieted some time ago. Fires burned low at the nearby wagons, and it appeared as if most everyone had gone to bed. It was peaceful again, now that the three young children were gone. Although, it had been surprisingly pleasant to have the kids in camp and watch Anna dote over them. She was a natural caretaker. Ethan took a long sip of his coffee.

"You look tired. Maybe you should get some rest," he suggested.

Anna laughed softly. She took a seat on one of the crates Ethan had set out for her before supper.

"Yes, I'm tired of Marybeth's constant talking." She raised her head to look up at him, a wide smile forming on her face. "I don't think anyone's ever put her in her place the way you did earlier."

Ethan knelt beside her and stared into the fire. "It's about time someone did," he mumbled. He'd put up with her, but he had to put a stop to the woman's suggestions that Anna marry Ed Howell.

"She won't let anyone get a word in, and if someone has an opinion, she has to argue how hers is better and correct." Anna's voice rose.

Ethan grinned. Seeing Anna get her hackles up, and not at him for a change, was a welcome sight. That familiar warm feeling he'd experienced with greater intensity since becoming aware of Anna, rushed through him again. The sudden need to pull her into his arms and kiss her was nearly unbearable.

"I thought you missed people to talk to and civilization. Isn't that one of the reasons you wanted to leave Harley's Hole?"

Anna stared at him. "You can wipe that satisfied smile off your face, Ethan Wilder." Her attempt to look stern faltered. She laughed, holding her hand over her mouth in an attempt to keep quiet. "Perhaps I forgot what it was like, and I don't miss it that much after all."

Ethan's chest tightened at the sight of her happiness. He hadn't ever seen her this radiant. She was like an alpine flower, blooming more as time passed. She reflected his own contentment.

Anna set her cup aside. "When I brought the children back to Ed's wagon, Marybeth told me you were rude for interrupting her." She chuckled as she spoke, her eyes meeting his.

"That woman is a piece of work. I don't know how any man, or the rest of her family puts up with her."

Ethan stood, pouring the rest of his coffee into the fire, dousing the flames and drowning them in a dark shadow. The hot coals hissed and smoked. He offered Anna his hand to help her to her feet. As she took a step away from the fire, her dress snagged on the crate on which she sat. She tugged, then lurched forward when it released. Ethan caught her around the waist. Anna's hands braced against his chest.

"I'm sorry," she whispered.

Rather than letting her go after she'd found her balance, his hold on her tightened. "I'm not," he murmured.

Her face was faint and difficult to make out. Ethan's hand searched for her cheek. His fingers ran up along her jaw to touch her lips, until his palm cupped the side of her face. Anna's breathing increased, judging by the rise and fall of her chest.

"Anna, I can't go on pretending to be your brother. I made a mistake. I can't keep fighting what my heart is telling me."

Ethan lowered his head, his lips against her cheek. He breathed in the faint scent of the soap she used to wash with each evening. The flowery fragrance on her skin was distinctly hers.

"I don't want you to pretend any longer that you're my brother, Ethan." Her soft whisper in the darkness was like a lightning strike to his heart, fully igniting the fire that had simmered inside him for her.

Ethan murmured her name right before his lips found hers. His right arm wrapped more fully around her waist, drawing her closer, while the other hand weaved into her hair, holding her to him.

Anna moaned softly, her lips parting beneath his. This time, he wasn't going to stop at a quick taste. He covered her mouth, fully savoring the softness of hers as she leaned into him. Her arms came around his neck, bringing him even closer. The world swirled into oblivion around him. There was nothing but the woman in his arms. Anna, whose gentle heart healed his damaged soul. Not even the loud screech coming from somewhere out of the darkness tore him out of her embrace.

"Oh, my Lord, what in heaven's name is going on here?"

Chapter Sixteen

"I knew right from the start that something wasn't as it should be between you two. I have a sense for these sort of things, you know."

Marybeth's screeching voice rang through the stillness of the evening air. Anna shrank away from Ethan, her heart pounding fiercely in her chest and in her head. She dropped her arms from around Ethan's neck, gulping in several breaths to steady her nerves, both from Marybeth's unexpected interruption as well as her reaction to Ethan's kiss. She tried to take a step back, but strong arms held her tight.

"I'm so sorry," she whispered against Ethan's solid chest, unsure if he could even hear over Marybeth's continued ranting. What was she sorry for? Certainly not Ethan's kiss, but definitely for the interruption to their private moment.

The woman must have eagle eyes if she was able to see them in the dark. Clearly, she'd come to their camp for a different reason. Anna wouldn't put it past her to want to eavesdrop. It was too dark to see much of anything, and only some orange coals glowed in the fire pit.

Faint light from lanterns that had been lit among the other wagons came toward them. Jeremy shouted in the distance for his wife.

"What's all the ruckus about?" Albert Howell wondered.

"I told you already, I ain't sorry." Ethan's deep voice came close to her ear.

He eased his hold on her when more people arrived in camp – Jeremy, Pastor Albert, Ed Howell, as well as Millicent and Maude's husbands along with Mildred.

"I came to give Anna my peach pie recipe, and to my great shock, I find Mr. Wilder overtaking and kissing his sister!" Marybeth didn't sound surprised, but rather triumphant at her juicy discovery. "I say it again. I've never seen a brother look at his sister the way Mr. Wilder looks at Anna. It's downright unnatural."

"What's going on here, Ethan?" Jeremy Howell stepped closer, holding up his lantern. Anna squinted when the light hit her eyes.

"Let me do the talking," Ethan said in a low tone. He stepped away from Anna to face Mr. Howell.

Anna caught the reassuring smile he had for her before his face faded into the shadows. He let go of her completely. Rather than answering, he bent to rekindle the campfire, instantly creating a circle of light around everyone.

Marybeth looked at her with wide eyes. "Well, it's clear what's going on, isn't it?" she said. "I've heard stories of men wanting to have their way with the women in their families. It's not talked about much, but I have eyes and ears, and I know these things. Why, back in Virginia –"

"Anna's not my sister," Ethan spoke loudly. He glared at the outspoken woman, then turned to Jeremy. Several of the men murmured.

"Well . . . well, of course I could have told you that," Marybeth stuttered. For once, she seemed to have run out of more words. "What do you mean, she's not your sister?" She stepped up to Anna. "What does he mean by that, Anna?"

"He means that he's not my brother," Anna stammered. "We're not related."

She looked to Ethan. He'd said to let him do the talking, but what was he going to say to these people? Regardless, they'd been caught in a most compromising situation.

158

Ethan returned to her and took her hand. He gave it a squeeze. His eyes silently pleaded with her to trust him. She nodded. He faced the men.

"Anna . . . Porter and I have known each other for the better part of a year. I met her as the close friend of my brother's wife. Although there is no familial relation between us, I, along with the rest of my brothers, regarded her as a sister."

He paused and glanced from one man to the next. Everyone stood and stared, waiting for him to continue.

"Well that doesn't explain what you were doing with her a few minutes ago. First you say she's your sister, then she's not, and now she's your sister again. Which one is it, Mr. Wilder?"

"Shush, for once, Marybeth," Jeremy spoke up.

Marybeth's hand shot to her hip. "I will not shush, Jeremy Howell. I have every right to know what's going on here. Anna's reputation is at stake, and I do believe -"

"Anna wanted to come to Oregon," Ethan said over Marybeth's protests. He stood tall in front of the men, looking as if he was ready to fight any one of them. He spoke loud enough to drown out Marybeth, but his voice remained steady.

"I agreed to bring her to Fort Hall. From there, I told her I'd accompany her to Oregon, to make sure she was safe."

"Well, of course she was safe. Are you insinuating that she wouldn't be safe with my family? This is the safest place she could be." Marybeth stood at Anna's side, offering her a sympathetic look. "If only we'd known from the beginning. I've been saying all along that she should marry Cousin Ed, then she'd have a man to take care of her. No need to try to deceive us. We don't take kindly to people lying to -"

"What I didn't want to admit at the time, to myself and - more importantly -to Anna Porter, is that over the course of several weeks prior to our leaving to come to Fort Hall, and during the journey there, she's earned my deepest respect."

Ethan looked at her, the light from the fire flickering in his eyes, which seemed to pierce right into her. He took a step closer, his fingers still wrapped tightly around hers. Anna locked her gaze on his. He'd never looked more serious, or more vulnerable at the same time as he did in that moment. When he spoke again, it was to her, and only her.

"Anna, I know I'm not the ideal man for you. I've been nothing but a surly old bear, but I do work hard, and I value my family. I'm willing to make a fresh start if you'll give me a chance."

Anna's eyes widened. A painful lump formed in her throat, preventing her from swallowing. Her head moved slowly from side to side.

"Ethan, what are you saying?" she whispered.

His voice grew louder, for everyone to hear. "What I didn't tell you before, was that I've come to care for you deeply, Anna." He took another small step toward her until their bodies nearly touched. "I've been a coward to admit it, but I can't deny it any longer. I've told myself countless times that I can't be drawn to you and then risk losing you. I'm starting to realize that it's a risk I want to take. I love you."

Anna blinked to dispel the moisture in her eyes. Lost for words, all she could do was stare, but Ethan's face became a blur. He'd just admitted he had feelings for her, words she'd wished he'd say to her. Murmurs erupted again from the men.

"I knew it!"

Anna shrank away from Marybeth's triumphant screech.

"We can't stand by and let these two continue to live in sin. What would people think? There's only one thing to do about it, isn't there?" Marybeth carried on. "What kind of man puts a sweet woman like Anna in such a scandalous position? Ed certainly would never have done that. He's far too honorable. In fact, I bet he would still marry her, even after this, this . . . disgrace."

Marybeth reached for Anna's arm, drawing her attention away from Ethan. He released her hand.

"This isn't what I would have done, Anna. I mean, if you would have married my cousin back home in Virginia, I would have arranged for a large wedding. I baked the grandest wedding cake once for my cousin Nellie. Of course, we can't do that here. But . . . "

Anna stared at Marybeth and shook her head. "I don't think getting married right now is –"

"Nonsense. It's the only solution. Someone needs to set things right. Your virtue has been compromised." She spun around. "Albert, you'll perform a wedding right now. It's the only way."

Anna pulled away from the overbearing woman. "Ethan?"

Ethan stepped in front of Marybeth. "I think, for once, Mrs. Howell is right." He grinned.

Anna's heart dropped to her stomach. Ethan agreed with Marybeth that she should marry Ed? Her eyes widened in confusion. No, he couldn't mean it. Not after the kiss they'd shared, and he'd just said he loved her.

"Of course I'm right, Mr. Wilder," Marybeth shot back. "Jeremy, go fetch Albert's Bible, so we can get Anna married. Who's it going to be? I'd like to get some sleep before the night's over."

Thankfully, she didn't wait for an answer, and moved away to take control of her husband and the other men, barking out orders on what everyone needed to do. She demanded they fetch their wives to be present at the wedding as witnesses.

"Maude can stay in her bed. She needs her rest."

"Ethan, this is crazy. What am I supposed to do?" Anna grabbed for his hand.

"I know what I'm going to do. I'm doing what's right, Anna, for both of us. It might be impulsive and reckless . . . and I might be acting for selfish reasons, but it's also the responsible thing to do." His face broke out in a wide grin. "Unless, of course, you'd rather marry Cousin Ed."

Anna snorted. "No, I don't want to marry Cousin Ed, but you –"

Ethan leaned down and silenced her with a kiss. He brushed his lips against hers, lingered for a moment, then pulled back.

"I'm not sure you heard me a minute ago over Marybeth's chatter." He held both her hands in his. "I love you, Anna Porter. I want to marry you. I don't think I've ever felt stronger about anything in my life."

Anna blinked. She had heard him the first time, but with Marybeth's incessant babbling, there had been no time to absorb his words. Ethan, who guarded his heart with the ferocity of a grizzly and feared getting attached to anyone, had just told her that he loved her. In front of a group of people, no less.

"Ethan, I . . . I love you, too."

The words slipped from her mouth, and having said them out loud, they were true beyond a doubt. She hadn't dared think them before, let alone say them, although her heart had already known weeks ago.

Ethan swept her in a tight embrace that knocked the air from her lungs and lifted her off her feet. His arms trembled as he held her close to him. The smile on his face, even in the shadows from the flickering campfire and several lanterns, erased all the hardness of his features.

"Will you marry me, Anna? I promise I'll –"

"Albert is ready to perform the ceremony," Marybeth called loudly. She clapped her hands together. "Anna have you decided who you are going to – oh, I see. Well, I guess you two should step forward, then."

Ethan groaned. He reluctantly released his hold around Anna and set her fully on her feet.

"Best do what she says," he murmured. "Or this might turn into a shotgun wedding. Has she said whether she's as good with a handgun as she claims to be with everything else?"

Anna breathed in a lungful of air and chuckled. "I don't know, and I'd rather not find out," she whispered.

Ethan led her to stand in front of Pastor Howell, who leafed through his Bible, then looked up, darting a glance from Anna to Ethan.

"This is the right thing to do," he said, shooting a stern look at Ethan.

Ethan nodded, his hand tightening around Anna's. "I agree."

She gazed up at him, staring at his profile. Ethan Wilder was going to be her husband. It seemed unreal. To think he had been the most unlikely person to bring her on this journey, and now she was taking a vow to be his wife. It seemed unthinkable that she could be this happy. She closed her eyes for a moment.

I love you Franklin, I always will. You will forever hold a special place in my heart, but I have to go on with my life. I know you'd be happy for me that I've found a good man with whom to spend the rest of my days.

"I'd understand, Miss Wilder, ah . . . Porter, if you'd prefer to marry Cousin Ed instead of Mr. Wilder. I could wed you to either one of these men this evening."

Anna's eyes flew open. She stared at the pastor, shaking her head. Turning to look at Ed, she said, "I'm sorry, but I love Ethan."

He nodded and smiled in understanding.

Ethan's hand closed tightly around hers. She squeezed back.

Pastor Howell cleared his throat. "Then I ask you, Anna Porter, do you take this man, Ethan Wilder, to be your husband? Do you –"

From behind them, Marybeth's loud whisper, no doubt intended for everyone to hear, drowned out what Pastor Howell said. "I would certainly have chosen a more reliable man, like Cousin Ed, but it's Anna's wedding, not mine."

Anna smiled into Ethan's eyes. Marybeth couldn't have been more wrong about his character.

"I take Ethan as my husband," she said when the pastor's mouth stopped moving and his forehead wrinkled in an inquisitive stare. He nodded in apparent satisfaction.

"Do you, Ethan Wilder, take this woman to be your wife? Do you –"

"I hope Mr. Wilder knows how to farm and grow crops. How is he going to provide for Anna once they get to Oregon? You'll have to teach him, Jeremy. We had the best farm in Virginia, and I know –"

"Shush, Marybeth, and let them get married," Jeremy warned.

"I will shush when I want to shush, Jeremy Howell. Don't you tell me –"

Ethan pulled Anna close and murmured against her cheek so she could hear, "I take you, Anna, as my wife."

"You are now man and wife," Pastor Howell proclaimed.

Ethan's eyes met hers, the usual hard lines of his features and the sullen look on his face were replaced with a satisfied smile. The rest of the people around them and Marybeth's chatter faded away. Anna's vision blurred as she stared up at him, love and contentment flowing through her. The hopes and dreams she'd had a year ago no longer mattered as she gazed into the eyes of her new husband, and the new direction her life would take from hereon.

Ethan leaned forward to kiss her lightly as his fingers caressed her cheek. "I suppose we're going to learn how to survive each other, aren't we?" he murmured against her lips.

Anna raised her head. The light from the lanterns faded away, leaving only the glow from the campfire around them. The chirping of countless crickets became louder as the sounds of the people drifted away. Even Marybeth's distinct voice faded away. They were alone.

"I think I was telling you to get some rest when I kissed you and got us both in trouble."

Ethan's voice filled the air around her. The orange light from the fire dimmed as the flames consumed the last of the wood, leaving behind glowing coals that flickered black one moment then erupted into red and orange light the next.

"Who would've thought that one kiss would lead to us being wed?" Anna murmured, trying to disguise the uncertainty in her voice.

Ethan chuckled. "With you, things seem to happen unexpectedly. I didn't think a bucket of dirty water in my face would wake me up to take notice of you."

"You were so angry that day," Anna giggled. "I thought for sure you were going to strangle me."

"My brothers always like to badger me, but no one's ever dressed me down like you did that day, and I couldn't stop thinking about you." Ethan pulled her into his arms. His chest heaved against hers. "You've pulled me out of my dark existence, Anna. I'm still not sure how you managed it, but you made me see that I'm ready to love someone."

Anna wrapped her arms around his neck. "I'm ready to move on from the past and love someone, too."

"You were right about me when you said I'm afraid of letting people get close to me, but what scares me more is the thought of losing someone I care about. I failed my parents when I didn't listen to my pa the day he died. It's a guilt I've lived with my whole life, because I was reckless and selfish. It's a pain I never want to feel again."

Anna touched his face, running her fingers against the roughness of his jaw. "We all worry about losing the ones we love, but you can't go through life with those kinds of fears. You won't be living if you do. You'll simply be miserable. I know I've been unhappy all this time, thinking about what might have happened differently had I acted differently."

She stood on her toes and kissed his lips. Ethan wrapped her fully into his arms and covered her mouth with his. Anna's limbs went weak, and she clung to him. Ethan bent forward, his lips still on hers, and swooped her up into his arms. Wrapping her own arms tightly around his neck to hold on, she met the sudden urgency of his kiss.

When he set her on the tailgate of the wagon, she was out of breath.

"I don't want to sleep under the wagon tonight," he whispered huskily against her neck.

Butterflies churned in her belly at his words.

"You're my husband. You don't have to anymore."

166

Ethan heaved himself into the wagon, pulling Anna with him into the dark confines of the rig's canvas-covered bed. The springs squeaked and the wagon rattled as they found each other in the darkness.

"Anna, I don't deserve your heart," Ethan murmured against the nape of her neck as he sat behind her on the straw mattress that had been her bed since leaving Harley's Hole.

He ran his hand down the back of her head, pulling out her hairpins as he went. When her braid fell down her back, he untied the ends and combed his fingers through her long strands.

Anna's heart beat wildly. This was her wedding night. With trembling fingers, she unhooked the buttons of her dress. Ethan helped her slip out of the bodice, his lips following along her exposed skin down her shoulder and arms.

"You're a good man, Ethan Wilder." A slight shiver passed through her once the dress was off and she wore nothing but her chemise. "You're the man I fell in love with."

Ethan turned her around, and her hands came in contact with the bare skin of his chest. When had he discarded his shirt? Her fingers explored along the taut muscles of his shoulders and arms. Memories of the day she'd last touched him like this filled in for not being able to see him in the dark.

"You've been the responsible one for so long. I think it's time you enjoyed life a little more," Anna mumbled, her lips touching his shoulders before she lifted her face to seek his mouth.

Ethan groaned, and eased her onto her back. "I think I'll take you up on that, Mrs. Wilder."

Her playful squeal was cut short when Ethan covered her mouth with his, pressing her into the mattress and fully claiming her lips. Arms and legs entwined as she explored and touched him, while Ethan did the same to her. When their bodies joined as one, a tear of joy escaped her eyes. Right here, in Ethan's arms, she'd finally found home.

Chapter Seventeen

The gray light of early morning filtered in through a small opening in the canvas at the back of the wagon. Ethan shifted his arm, but was stopped short by the weight of Anna's head resting against the crook of his shoulder. A content smile widened his mouth, followed quickly by a cold rush of dread.

Anna was his wife. He'd finally admitted his feelings not only to her, but to himself last night. For a dozen years, he'd sworn never to do anything impulsive again, yet marrying her on the spot had taken less thought than anything else he'd ever experienced. He'd never wanted anything as much as having Anna for his wife even though he'd fought against emotional attachments for more than half his life.

Ethan stroked her cheek. His arm tightened around the sleeping woman, bringing her closer against him. The familiar painful feeling of loss and guilt swept over him again. He gritted his teeth and mentally shook his head. He wasn't going to lose Anna. He wasn't going to make the same mistakes he'd made in the past.

She'd taught him to open his heart and move beyond all his remorse and fears. He wasn't going to start the first day of their new life together wallowing in dread. His mother and father would have been happy for him for finding a woman like Anna.

Anna's eyes opened, and she blinked, looking up at him. When she smiled, any doubts melted away instantly. He tugged her up closer, and kissed her forehead.

"Good morning, Mrs. Wilder," he murmured.

"Goodness, I think we slept too long." Anna squinted toward the light coming from outside.

Ethan chuckled. "I don't think we slept enough."

Her face turned scarlet at his words and she dropped her gaze, pulling the blanket that laid over them up past her exposed shoulder. Ethan gently pushed the covering away, and rubbed his hand down her arm, then along the curve of her hips and thighs, eliciting a soft moan from her.

"What's Cora going to say when she finds out she and I are truly sisters now?" Anna whispered, sliding her palm against his bare chest.

Ethan sucked in a quick breath at his body's reaction to her innocent movement. He shifted from his back to his side, pulling Anna close. His hand cupped her cheek, then slid up into her hair, brushing back strands that had fallen into her face. His eyes roamed over her, still awed by the thought that she belonged to him, and the feeling of pure happiness that flowed through him. When had he ever felt this content?

"Does that mean you want to return to Harley's Hole?" he murmured into her hair, his lips gliding along her forehead. "Or are you planning to send a letter from Oregon?"

Anna braced against him and looked up into his eyes. "I found what I've been searching for, Ethan." Her finger grazed along his chest. "It's you, and wherever you are, that's where I want to be. Harley's Hole is your home, and honestly, I miss it, too."

Ethan chuckled. "Good, since I don't think I recall how to plow a field and grow a crop. I've lived in the woods too long. Marybeth would be disappointed in me."

Anna laughed and leaned forward to kiss his lips. "Marybeth is always disappointed with something. Besides, she isn't your wife, whom you have to please." A glimmer of mischief sparkled in her eyes.

170

"Thank God for that." Ethan pulled her into his arms and rolled her onto her back, silencing her laughter with his mouth.

He shifted his weight to deepen the kiss when the loud and distinctly grating voice of Marybeth Howell screeched outside. Ethan groaned and slumped to the side. Anna's body vibrated underneath him with laughter. He wrapped her tightly in his arms and joined in.

"What are you talking about, Albert Howell? That's impossible." Her voice drew closer to the wagon. "And where are Anna and Mr. Wilder? Their cooking fire isn't even lit."

A man coughed loudly. "Perhaps they had a long night," Jeremy suggested.

"Well, the day's going to waste away if we don't start early," she proclaimed. Her voice sounded as if she was right on the other side of the canvas. "Anna? Are you in there, Anna?"

Anna startled at the sudden pounding on the outside of the wagon. She extracted her head from under Ethan's chest. "I'm getting dressed, Marybeth," she called, her voice muffled. "I'll be out in a moment."

"Well, you'd better, and find that husband of yours. Jeremy and the others seem to think the mules and oxen have wandered off."

Anna looked up into Ethan's eyes, frowning.

"Grazing is sparse here," Ethan said quietly. "It's been getting worse the further we've traveled. The animals may have wandered in the night to look for food. Whoever was on watch should have kept a better lookout." He reached for his britches and shirt. "I'd better go and help find them."

Ethan dressed quickly, then pulled Anna into his arms one final time and kissed her with the promise of continuing their honeymoon later, then hopped from the

171

wagon. Marybeth Howell's eyes widened when he emerged.

"Why aren't you out looking for the livestock, Mr. Wilder?" she chided. "Without the mules and oxen, we can't start the day, now can we? I tell you, laziness was never tolerated back home in Virginia. Everyone was up before the rooster crowed."

Ethan ignored the woman and sought out Jeremy Howell. He stood over a campfire by his wagon, sipping a cup of coffee. He appeared to be deep in thought. He looked up when Ethan approached.

"Who had early morning watch?"

Jeremy rubbed his hand across the back of his neck while he looked Ethan in the eye. "One of the scouts. I believe Anton. Cousin Ed had first watch, then Sabin took over for him."

"Have you talked to Anton?"

Jeremy slurped from his coffee mug, looking away. "No one has seen either Anton or Sabin since last night," he said slowly in a quiet voice.

"What?"

Anger mixed with understanding. Ethan cursed under his breath. Ever since leaving Fort Hall, he'd kept a close eye on those two scouts. He'd reasoned with himself over and over again that men who lived in the mountains didn't always look presentable. Even so, there had been something about Oliver Sabin that had set off warning bells in his head.

The one night he should have been vigilant, he'd spent in the arms of his wife, completely oblivious to anything that went on around him.

"Maybe they've gone looking for the livestock before anyone else noticed," Jeremy suggested.

Ethan scoffed. "You don't believe that any more than I do. I should have known better, and suggested you hire someone else while we were still at Fort Hall."

Jeremy's eyes widened. "You think they stole the livestock?"

Ethan nodded. "And you believe it, too. I can see it in your eyes. We'll organize a search near camp, but my hunch is those animals are miles away from here by now."

Jeremy stared at him as if someone had died. "Without the oxen and mules, we're stuck here. What are we going to do?"

Ethan shrugged. "There's not much water here, but we should be all right until the next outfit passes by. Maybe you or someone else can barter for a horse from them and ride back to Fort Hall for help."

Hell. He should do it himself, but the thought of leaving the wagons and Anna sent a shiver down his spine. He'd done that once before, and it had ended in tragedy. Right now, the best thing to do was stay here and wait for someone else to pass through while continuing to look for their livestock, although that seemed like a futile idea.

Jeremy shook his head. "There won't be any other wagons coming this way."

Ethan frowned. "There were several outfits heading out a day after us from Fort Hall. They can't be too far behind."

Jeremy lowered his head. He shook it, then let out a drawn-out sigh. Whatever he was about to say next would not be good news. Ethan braced for the worst.

"When we were at Fort Hall, Oliver Sabin told us he knew of a shortcut off the main trail that would save us several weeks of travel. He said he'd been in the area plenty of times, and knew the way like the back of his hand. He even told me he wouldn't take any payment from us until we reached Fort Boise."

Ethan gritted his teeth. "And when did we break off from the main trail?" His words were low and quiet, while his insides threatened to boil with rage. These people had been swindled, and he hadn't seen it. This was unfamiliar territory to him, and he hadn't paid attention because he'd been too preoccupied with other thoughts. Being stranded in the middle of nowhere might cost them their lives.

"Three days ago." Jeremy tossed the rest of his coffee into the fire and stared up at the sky. "How could I have let this happen?"

"Jeremy!" Marybeth Howell stormed in their direction.

"Control your wife, Howell. I need to think about what we're going to do without worrying everyone," Ethan warned.

Jeremy's eyes filled with hope. "Having you here eases my concerns, Ethan. You're a woodsman like those other two. You can get us out of this."

Ethan's hand curled into a fist. "I might be a woodsman, but I ain't like those two thieves."

"That's certainly not what I meant to imply. You know your way around –"

"Jeremy, Albert says there is no sign of the livestock anywhere." Marybeth sauntered toward her husband. She shot a stern look at Ethan, then ignored him. "Do you want to know what I think? I think Indians came and took them. That's the only thing that makes sense. They'll be coming for us next."

"Indians don't steal mules," Ethan said quietly. "They have no use for them."

"What do you mean, they have no use for them? Everyone has use for mules."

Marybeth turned on him, her eyes blazing with annoyance for him having contradicted her. Ed, Albert, and the husbands of Millicent and Maude headed their

174

way. Anna followed with the women, staying close beside Maude, whose advanced pregnancy prevented her from moving fast.

Anna came to his side and slipped her hand in his, glancing at him with a silent question. Ethan waited for Jeremy to speak, but the man shot him a pleading look. Ethan straightened. Apparently he was the one who would break the bad news to the families.

"I haven't gone to search for tracks, but from what I believe, the livestock were herded away in the night by our scouts, Anton and Sabin."

A loud murmur erupted among the five men. One of the women gasped.

"Why would they do that?" Anna asked softly.

"I'm telling you, it was Indians. They've probably been following us for days. Most likely they killed our scouts."

Ethan ignored Marybeth. He looked around at the faces staring at him. These people were helpless in the wilderness. Without a proper guide, they'd never get out of this predicament on their own.

"Indians might steal a cow or an ox and the horses, but they'd leave mules behind. Since Sabin and Anton are missing, it's not hard to figure out what happened. They led you on the wrong trail so they could take your animals, most likely to sell them at Fort Hall or somewhere else."

"What will happen to us?"

"Some of the men will have to walk to the main trail, and wait for help to come along."

Marybeth laughed a shrill laugh. "You can't be serious, Mr. Wilder. We can't split up like that."

"You may not have a choice."

Ethan looked at the families around him. Ed held his youngest girl in his arms. Millicent consoled her crying youngster. Maude stood, her hands clutching her swollen belly. These people might not survive. His gaze drifted to

175

Anna. He wasn't going to leave her. Jeremy and a couple of the others would have to head back to the main trail, while he'd remain behind and wait.

The thought barely crossed his mind, when Maude cried out. She bent forward, gripping at her stomach. Mildred and Marybeth rushed to her side while her husband stumbled back, his eyes wide with worry. Anna rushed up to her.

"Let's get her to her wagon," she said. "She's in labor."

"Lord in heaven, what next? It seems that there is no end to our disasters lately. I wouldn't be surprised if those Indians come and scalp us in our sleep. Not that birthing a baby is a tragedy. It's just the timing of it all. When I had my babies in Virginia, it was the easiest thing in the world. Good thing I'm here to help deliver this one. Come along, Maude, you're going to be fine. Let's get you to your wagon."

Anna stayed behind while the other women helped Maude to her rig. Ethan raked his hand through his hair. The responsibility for these people had fallen on him, and he had no answers as to what to do.

The men huddled around Jeremy, who looked toward Ethan.

"We'll figure out what to do once I take a look at the tracks." He headed for Anna's wagon and pulled his rifle out from the bed.

Anna came up beside him. She reached for his shoulder. Ethan forced a smile, his eyes roaming over the woman who calmed the turmoil inside him.

"What are you thinking?" she whispered.

He opened his arms, and she stepped into his embrace.

"I don't know how to keep you safe and get everyone out of here," he murmured against her hair.

"Yes you do." She raised her head. Trust shimmered in her eyes when she smiled up at him.

"We're three days' walk from the main trail and the possibility of finding help, according to Jeremy." He released her and kicked at the dirt on the ground, sending up a swirl of dust.

"Dammit!" Ethan raked his hand through his hair. "Why was I so careless? I should have realized we were off the main trail."

A short distance away, a scream came from inside Maude's wagon. Marybeth's shrill voice followed. Ethan tensed. Anna reached for his arm, looking up at him with soft eyes.

"This isn't your fault, Ethan. When we were with our company from Independence, the scouts recommended a cut-off that we took that saved us several days to Fort Laramie. It's not uncommon."

"But I should have seen right through that crook, Sabin. I could smell he was trouble back at Fort Hall."

"You can't bear the responsibility for this, Ethan. This was Jeremy's decision." She wrapped her arms around his middle.

Ethan held her tight. His arms trembled while his mind churned with indecision.

"You know what you have to do, Ethan," Anna whispered against his chest. "You're the only one here who knows how to track."

Ethan tensed. "What are you saying?" He didn't need to ask for clarity because he'd thought the same thing.

"You can find the livestock, and at least get your horse back. Then you can ride for help. It's the fastest solution. We can't stay out here in the middle of nowhere for very long."

Ethan grabbed her by the arms and stared down at her. "I'm not leaving you," he growled.

Anna reached her hand up to touch his face. "I know what's on your mind. This is not like the last time, when you left your parents' wagon and went off on your own. This time, you're doing it to save the rest of us."

Ethan stared at her. She was right, but how could he risk leaving her? He couldn't protect her if he left the wagons.

"You have to go. The longer you wait, the further away Sabin is going to get."

"Anna," he mumbled. He leaned forward and kissed her soft lips. "I love you. Last night when you became my wife, I swore to myself that I would never let anything happen to you."

"There are five other wagons here, and the other men." She laughed softly. "And we have Marybeth. She alone would scare anyone away."

Ethan grinned for the first time. "You have a good point."

"You know this is the only way. You have to do this. We'll be fine until you return."

Maude cried out again at that moment. Ethan glanced to the direction of the wagon, then back to Anna. His lips set in a firm line.

"I'll be back before dark, whether I find the animals or not."

Anna clasped his face between her hands and kissed him. He pulled her into his arms, unwilling to let her go, but he had to. This was surely the hardest decision of his life. Slowly, he eased away from the woman who meant everything to him. He nodded, then reached for his rifle, and set off in the direction where he'd left his horse to graze the night before.

* * * * *

Ethan ran across the wide expanse of the prairie, dodging larger sage shrubs while keeping his eyes focused on the ground. The tracks led west, and were easy to follow in most places, while in others, the terrain was uneven and rocky. The black rocks in this landscape looked unusual but were reminiscent of some of the formations he'd seen in Yellowstone country.

By the time the sun had moved well past the zenith, Ethan slowed to take a drink from his canteen. Water was nowhere to be found here in this desolate area. The wind blew hot in his face as he swiped the sweat off his forehead. Squinting into the distance, a large stand of trees loomed on the horizon. Ethan corked his canteen and set off again.

No doubt Anton and Sabin had driven the livestock as far away as possible, thinking no one would follow them. They would most likely take the animals to the next trading post to sell to emigrants who were in need of fresh animals. This was probably not the first time they'd hired on as scouts and led a group of travelers astray and stolen their animals. They would then most likely go back and rob them again, once the families were desperate and had no choice but to abandon their wagons and set out on foot."

As he neared the trees, it became obvious that his hunch had been right. A group of oxen, cattle, and mules, along with several horses picked at the sparse vegetation that grew in this area. Shrubs had been used to create a make-shift enclosure. Ethan slowed his approach. Other than vegetation, there was no place to take cover. There was also no sign of Anton or Sabin.

Ethan circled the small herd, using the animals to conceal himself. Satisfied that the thieves weren't present, he searched out his horse. The lead rope dangled from its halter. He patted the animal's neck, then led the gelding from the enclosure.

Where were Anton and Sabin? Ethan scoured the ground for more tracks. Two sets of hoof prints in the soil heading east sent a cold wave of dread down his spine. Gripping his rifle, he leapt onto his horse's back and nudged the animal into a gallop, pointing him to where he'd left the wagons . . . and Anna.

Chapter Eighteen

Using the corner of her apron to grab ahold of the handle, Anna lifted a boiling kettle of water from the fire and carried it to Maude's wagon. The young woman's screams of pain had increased in the last couple of hours. Mildred had predicted that it wouldn't be much longer for the baby to arrive.

"I didn't have this much trouble delivering my two young'uns," Marybeth announced. "They just slid right out. Maybe she's not pushing hard enough."

"Please hand me that wash basin, so I can pour the water into it," Anna said to distract Marybeth. Her constant commentary surely wasn't helping poor Maude, or her husband. The nervous man paced along the edge of their camp, his face pale and distraught.

"Don't pour that water, yet. I've got a cleaner basin in my wagon, Anna." Marybeth made a face as she peered into the washbasin Anna had taken from Maude's supplies, and snatched it away and set it on the ground before Anna had the chance to pour the water. Her arms ached from holding the heavy kettle.

"Yes, Miss Know-it-all," Anna mumbled under her breath when Marybeth was out of earshot. Why did she put up with her deplorable behavior, like everyone else? It was simply easier to let her carry on than constantly fret about it.

She set the kettle on the tailgate and swiped her hair out of her face. After Ethan had left earlier, she'd braided it into a quick rope and tied a kerchief around it to keep the dust off her head.

Anna straightened and held her hand to her lower back. The sun shone brightly overhead, already past its highest point. Maude had been in labor since early morning, her cries of pain piercing through the otherwise still prairie.

Earlier, Marybeth had insisted that Jeremy and some of the men go in search of the oxen, leaving only Maude's husband and Pastor Howell in camp, along with the women and children. Thankfully, Millicent kept all the kids entertained at her wagon.

"There's no sense everyone sitting around with nothing to do," Marybeth had proclaimed. "Mr. Wilder is only one man. He can't find the livestock all by himself. And I still say it was Indians who took them. Maude's husband should stay here, and let's have Albert stay with us, too. The rest of you men go and help find those animals."

"I don't think it's a good idea," Anna had said. "If anyone can find them, Ethan will. He can track anything in the mountains and I'm sure he's –"

"Nonsense, Anna. The more people we have out looking, the faster we'll have the animals back and we can be on our way."

Anna shook her head when Marybeth once again had to have it her way. Her husband probably obliged her and left camp simply to get some reprieve from his wife. She'd never wanted to think badly about anyone, but this woman sent her over the edge and really tested her patience.

Ethan was completely correct. How could anyone put up with her for an extended period of time? No doubt Marybeth meant well, but she needed someone to put her in her place. Anna smiled.

Ethan hadn't had any problems doing that. Marybeth may not have even been aware of the subtle way Ethan dealt with the woman. She didn't like Ethan, probably because she knew he wouldn't play to her tune.

"We'll need that water soon," Mildred called from inside the wagon.

"Just a minute."

Anna reached for the discarded basin that hadn't been good enough for Marybeth. Since the woman hadn't come back yet with the one she deemed much better, Anna wiped out the one at her disposal, then poured some hot water into it. Inside the wagon, Maude screamed. A second later, the loud wail of a newborn pierced the air.

Anna peered into the wagon, setting the basin on the ground next to Mildred, who held up the crying newborn.

"She's got a strapping boy," Mildred announced, a wide smile on her face. "You can send the proud new father over in a few minutes, Anna. Just let me clean the baby up a bit."

Anna left to find Maude's husband, who still paced at the outskirts of camp. He shot an anxious look her way when Anna waved to him.

"You can go and see your wife and baby in a minute," she said. His face lit up in a wide smile and he thanked her, then rushed to camp.

Anna smiled, staring after him. Perhaps someday Ethan would wear the pleased smile of a proud new father, too. Turning to head back to the wagons, she thought better of it when Marybeth rushed through camp, barking something at the poor man. She changed course to walk behind the wagons and out of camp.

Anna shook her head. She stood with her arms wrapped around her middle and stared out at the vast prairie. A mild breeze blew warm air in her face, and she closed her eyes. Ethan would be back soon. There was no doubt he would find the livestock.

A shiver passed through her as apprehension grabbed her. How would he get the animals back from the thieves? She shook it off. Ethan was as confident in the mountains as those two lowlifes. And they didn't know he was coming. No sooner had she thought it when a shot rang through the air, followed by Marybeth's loud scream.

Anna spun on her heels, her eyes darting toward camp. The thunder of hoof beats sounded in the distance as two men came galloping toward the wagons. One held a rifle in his hand, ready to fire.

"He's been shot," Marybeth screeched. "Lord, he's been shot."

"Oh, no." Anna ran toward camp. On the ground by Mildred's wagon was Pastor Albert, clutching at his arm. The burly man sat against one of the wagon wheels, gasping for air.

"Albert?" Mildred's frantic call came from the wagon where Maude had recently given birth. She climbed from the back of the rig and ran to her husband.

The two men on horseback had almost reached the wagons. Anna ran for her rig. She reached it at the same moment the men rode into camp. There was a spare pistol somewhere in the bed.

"Don't anyone move," the man with the eye patch called out. His rifle was pointed at Marybeth, who knelt by Pastor Albert. A chill raced down Anna's spine at his cold, sinister voice.

She darted behind her wagon, her heart pounding against her ribs. If Sabin and Anton had returned, where was Ethan?

"I want to know what the meaning of this is," Marybeth called loudly. "You desert us, then you come back and shoot Pastor Albert. You just wait until my husband gets back."

"Yore the first one we're gonna kill if ya don't stop yer jawin', woman. Had about enough o' ya in the last week. Plumb drive a man to kill hisself." Sabin pointed his rifle at Marybeth. Her mouth flew open and she gasped. Sabin laughed.

"Everyone get out of yore wagons so we can see ya," Sabin shouted. "Or this woman gets a bullet between her eyes."

"Maude just gave birth," Pastor Albert rasped from where he sat on the ground. His face was doused in sweat and his breathing labored. "She can't leave her wagon."

Millicent climbed from the back of her wagon and helped the children down. Anton pointed his gun at all of them and motioned for them to sit on the ground with the pastor. One of the little girls began to cry. Anton stuck his head inside Maude's wagon, then yelled for her husband to get out. He grabbed the man by the shirt collar and shoved him roughly toward the others. Maude frantically called his name.

"If ya don't stay quiet, I'll drag ya out, too," Anton warned.

"Please, don't hurt us. We'll give you whatever you want," Marybeth cried.

Sabin laughed coldly. "Oh, I know ya will. I ain't asking. I'm just here ta take it. Let's start with yore things. Go fetch all the coins and silverware ya got from yore wagon, woman."

Sabin fired off a shot directly at her feet, sending up dirt and dust. Marybeth screamed, then ran for her wagon.

"Where are the others?" Sabin demanded.

"The men have gone looking for our livestock," Pastor Albert answered, glancing around. Even from a distance, his eyes appeared clouded with pain.

Anna crept to the back of her wagon while keeping her eye on the two men. They hadn't seen her, yet. Slowly, she reached inside, groping for the pistol. Her hand made contact with her butcher knife instead. Her fingers curled around the handle once she touched cold steel. Quickly, she snatched the knife from the wagon and buried it under her apron.

"Hey, there's another woman over there," Sabin shouted. He fired his rifle. The shot splintered the wood near Anna's head. She shrieked and ducked out of the way. A quiet curse escaped her lips as her heart dropped to her stomach.

The other man, Anton, rushed to her and grabbed Anna by the arm.

"Don't try and hide. I've had my eye on you since we left Fort Hall."

Anna squeezed her eyes shut as his hot breath grazed her cheek. She gagged at the stench coming from the man's mouth.

"My husband will kill you," she sneered, stumbling next to him as he dragged her away from the wagon. Anton laughed.

"So sorry we wasn't invited to the weddin' last night. Looks like ya gonna have a short marriage."

He tore the kerchief from her head and dipped it into the nearest fire. He tossed it into the back of her wagon.

"No," she cried, her eyes widening. She pulled away from him. "Everything I own is in that wagon. All my memories." Tears ran down her face as the canvas of her rig caught fire, sending up smoke and flames.

"Don't worry, darlin'. We'll make new memories." Anton laughed in her ear.

"Bring her over here," Sabin ordered. He dismounted his horse. His one eye gleamed with pure evil as Anton shoved her in front of him.

"Go tie everyone up, so they can rot when we leave," Sabin ordered his accomplice. "While I have a talk with this one." He never took his eye off Anna.

She swallowed down the fear that ripped through her. Standing tall, she squared her shoulders and lifted her chin. She was not going to cower to this evil man. Since her journey west had started over a year ago, she'd considered herself unfit for the harshness of the trip. Ethan had also regarded her as weak at one point.

This was her chance to prove to herself that she wasn't weak. She might die, but she wouldn't die begging for her life. Her only regret was that she'd never see her husband again.

He might be dead, too.

Sabin continued to stare at her. He smiled, making his one eye gleam even colder. "I've waited twenty long years for one special moment," he said, his voice sending a chill down Anna's spine. "And I have you to thank for making it happen . . . soon."

"You're insane," Anna hissed. "I have no idea what you're talking about." She pulled the knife out from under her apron, the steel blade inches from Sabin's face.

Quicker than a snake striking out at her, Sabin grabbed her wrist. He twisted her arm until she dropped her weapon. Anna cried out in pain. The smile on Sabin's face turned into a murderous leer.

"Should I tell ya what happened to the last person who used a knife on me?"

Anna sucked in several breaths. "If you're going to kill me, then get it over with," she said boldly. Behind her, the fire of her burning wagon crackled and spit.

Sabin's laughter pierced the air. While still holding tight to her wrist, he bent to pick up the knife she'd dropped. He held it up, turning it in his hand and studying the reflection of the sun on the blade.

"A little dull," he said. "That'll hurt more." He held the cold steel to the pulse throbbing in her neck, sliding it along her skin. Anna leaned her head back in an attempt to avoid the weapon.

"You're nothing but a vile and evil coward," she said through gritted teeth, staring into his good eye.

Sabin roared with laughter, then in the next instant, twisted her arm behind her back and spun her around. Anna pressed her lips together to suppress a cry of pain.

"You all get to see what's going to happen to this pretty lady if you don't cooperate. If anyone so much as blinks, she dies. Where's that loud-mouthed woman I told ta get her coins?"

Anton rushed to Marybeth's wagon and pulled her out. She screeched and squawked like a chicken on the butcher block as he dragged her through camp and tied her up with the others.

Sabin pushed Anna in front of him, keeping the knife held to her throat. She could barely breathe from the foul odor coming from the man holding her tightly against his chest, her arm pressed between them.

Anna glimpsed her wagon, which was now fully engulfed in flames. Several pieces of canvas fluttered in the breeze, and one landed on one of the other wagons. Millicent cried out.

"Anna," a child's voice called.

Anna strained her eyes to see little Hattie poke her head out of the wagon that had just caught fire.

"Dear God, no." Anna gasped. "Please, someone get her out of there." She turned her head as far as it would go, straining against the tight hold Sabin had on her. The blade of her knife pressed harder against her neck. "Please, she's just a baby."

Millicent cried, as did Mildred. Pastor Albert pleaded for Anton to have mercy on a little child. He strained against the rope that tied him to the wagon wheel. Anton simply laughed. He headed for the wagon that had caught fire when a shot rang out. The trapper dropped like a fly and lay dead on the ground. Behind Anna, Sabin cursed loudly. He gripped her tighter, pushing her toward his horse.

Anna strained her eyes to look around frantically without moving her neck. Off in the distance, a lone rider galloped toward them. His rifle was raised, but he didn't shoot.

"Ethan," she whispered. He was alive and he'd come back!

Sabin held her firmly in front of him, clearly using her as a shield. Anna struggled, kicking at the rifle that lay on the ground when they reached his horse. The weapon slid out of his reach.

Sabin cursed loudly as Anna fought to get away. By the sound of the horse's hooves, Ethan was almost to camp. The outlaw must have realized it, too. He shoved her roughly to the ground and jumped into the saddle, leaning to the side of his horse.

"Anna stay down," Ethan yelled. Another shot rang out.

Anna raised her head. She scrambled to her feet.

"Hattie," she yelled. "Ethan, please save Hattie."

Ethan must have heard her. Rather than following Sabin, his horse thundered past her to the wagon where the little girl was trapped. Sabin had kicked his horse into a run, creating a cloud of dust in his wake. Hattie's cries grew louder over the spitting of the fire.

Ethan leapt from his mount and up into the wagon. He disappeared beneath the canvas that had erupted fully in flames, only to emerge seconds later, carrying the little girl. Anna's limbs barely supported her as she ran toward him.

"Ethan," she cried as she fell into his arms, little Hattie between them.

"It's all right. I've got you," he murmured, his voice weak with relief. His arms trembled as he held her close. "I've got you."

"Someone please untie us," Marybeth pleaded, her voice unusually weak.

Anna stepped out of Ethan's embrace. The look in his eyes was a mixture of anguish and relief. In the next instant, cold fury darkened his gaze. He stared off into the distance in the direction where Sabin had escaped. Ethan's body tensed.

"He's not worth going after," Anna said, touching his arm. "Pastor Albert's been shot. You're needed here, not chasing after that vile man."

"He won't be back. Men like that are too cowardly. If I ever cross paths with him again, I will kill him." Ethan's gaze returned to her. "He almost took the most important thing in my life away from me."

"But you came back just in time, and you saved both me and little Hattie, too." Tears rolled down Anna's cheeks, smiling at Ethan for reassurance. It was probably best not to let him see the fear that still swept through her. Everything was going to be all right now.

Marybeth screeched louder for someone to untie her. Ethan pulled his knife from his belt and headed for the people bound to the wagon.

* * * * *

Jeremy shook Ethan's hand, pumping it vigorously up and down. "You're sure you're not going to continue on with us?"

Ethan shook his head and glanced toward Anna, who sat waiting on the horse for which he'd traded their team of mules.

"My wife and I are heading home. Oregon's not the right place for us."

Jeremy nodded in understanding. "Sure would've been nice to have you with us. You're a good man."

Ethan laughed. "I think you'll do just fine with the outfit you've joined. There's safety in numbers, and they've got some good, reliable guides."

"If you say they're reliable, then I believe you. All the best to you."

Ethan nodded a final time, then led his horse toward Anna. It was time to get home to Harley's Hole. He stepped into the stirrup and swung up into the saddle.

He grinned. "Ready to head home and explain to the family why you've decided to come back?"

"I'll let you explain to Cora why I'm now her sister-in-law, and that –"

"Anna, wait, you can't leave just yet."

Ethan groaned. He didn't have to look over his shoulder to see whose screeching voice grew louder behind him.

"I was hoping to be gone before she saw us," he grumbled. "Didn't you say your goodbyes to everyone?"

"I did." Anna smiled. She waved at Marybeth, who came rushing to her horse's side.

"I wanted to give something to you, Anna. I couldn't possibly let you leave without it." She held up a package wrapped in cloth.

"Thank you," Anna said, her eyes filled with surprise.

"It's my special corn bread. Baked it just last night. You'll be getting hungry on your journey back to Fort Hall, no doubt. Wouldn't want you to leave without having tasted my cornbread. You know it's won several prizes back home in Virginia, so you know it'll be good. Although, it was a bit difficult to make in the campfire. My stove in Virginia was so much better."

"I'm sure Ethan and I will enjoy it very much." Anna handed Ethan the parcel. "Won't we, Ethan?" Her eyes widened, and she nudged her head toward Marybeth.

"Yeah, thanks. It smells good."

Anna held her hand to her mouth. She seemed to quickly regain her composure and leaned forward over the saddle, offering Marybeth her hand.

"Have a safe journey to Oregon."

"Oh, and you, too. Safe journey to . . . wherever it is you're going."

Anna glanced at Ethan. "My home is in Harley's Hole on the west side of the Teton Mountains. It's beautiful there."

"I'm sure it is, but probably not as nice as Virginia."

"We should get going, Anna," Ethan urged.

"You really need to tell that husband of yours not to order you around so much," Marybeth huffed.

Anna laughed. "I'll be sure and remind him. Take care, Marybeth."

She nudged her horse into a walk, away from the dozen wagons camped along the trail that overlooked the Snake River. Ethan reined his horse to fall in step next to hers. Finally, they could be on their way home. On horseback, it would take a little more than two weeks.

Ethan was eager to get back, although he already bristled at the badgering he'd get from his brothers. No doubt Harley would be hopping from one foot to the other with joy. Somehow, it seemed as if the old man had already known that Anna was the one for him.

"I hope they make it safely to Oregon from here with no more mishaps along their journey."

Ethan chuckled. "Every new start begins with mishaps. Look at how it started for us." He glanced at his wife and grinned. "I just hope we're done with them for a while."

"I suppose that means you won't want to try a new tea I've been meaning to brew."

Anna laughed at the scowl Ethan shot her. It quickly turned into a smile.

"I'm glad the Howells joined the Benson outfit," she said to change the subject. "It's like you told Jeremy – safety in numbers."

"I think they'll be just fine."

Five days had passed since that awful day when Ethan had thought his life was replaying itself from when he was a boy. When he'd realized that Sabin and Anton had been on their way back to the wagons, terror had consumed him. When he'd seen the smoke in the distance and then the burning wagons, he'd been certain his worst fears had come true.

He'd never been more relieved and grateful when he'd found Anna alive, but the thought of Sabin at large somewhere made anger boil inside him. Someday, the evil man would cross paths with the wrong person, and he'd get what he deserved.

Jeremy and the other men had returned to camp after seeing all the smoke, as Ethan was removing a bullet from Pastor Albert's arm. Ethan told the men exactly where to find the livestock. Jeremy had set out the following morning with two others to bring the animals back, while Ethan had stayed behind to guard the wagons and keep everyone safe.

This morning, they'd returned to the main trail and met up with the Benson outfit, who had agreed to join together with the Howells.

"I wonder if Benson will be as happy about his decision to allow them to come along once he gets a full taste of Marybeth Howell." Ethan glanced at Anna, who laughed.

"You mean, once he gets a taste of Marybeth's corn chowder and corn bread. It's the best in all of Virginia, but not quite as good as she makes it back home, you know."

Ethan chuckled and reached for Anna's hand as they rode in the direction of Harley's Hole.

"I'll be glad to get your biscuits again when we get home, Anna Wilder, because they're the best anywhere."

The saddle leather creaked when he leaned toward her for a kiss. She gazed into his eyes when he drew back. The love reflecting in them melted his insides.

"You're an incredible man, Ethan Wilder," she whispered. "And I love you."

Ethan squeezed her hand. "You have the biggest, most helpful heart of anyone I know, Anna, and you melted mine. I'm thankful every day that you've made me see what it's like to love, and that you gave your heart to me."

Epilogue

"It sure was nice of Harley to let us have the cabin tonight. It feels good to sleep in a real bed again after all those weeks on the trail."

Anna snuggled closer to Ethan in his bunk. She wrapped her arm around his middle and smiled up at him.

"Travis and Trevor aren't too happy that I kicked them to the barn, but that's what they get for giving me so much sass." Ethan kissed her forehead. His hand slid along her bare arm, sending shivers of delight down Anna's spine.

"Travis had a worried look on his face, did you notice?" Anna's smile widened. "After it finally sunk in that you and I are married, they both looked at me like I'd completely lost my mind. I think it's going to take them a while to get used to the new you."

"At least I won't have to put up with them for a while since I'll be sending them to Fort Hall for supplies in a few weeks. Why do you think Travis looked worried?"

Anna giggled. "Because you're the second brother to get married in less than a year. I know he and Trevor are still very young, but I'm sure it's going through his mind that Harley is going to badger them in a few years to find wives, too."

Ethan chuckled. "Travis is going to have a lot of growing up to do before any woman is gonna want him. I don't see that happening any time soon. He still needs a good cuff behind the ears every once in a while."

Anna shrugged. "Who knows, someone is bound to tame him, and then he'll change."

"A good woman sure made a difference in me."

195

Anna smiled. "Things sure seem to be changing fast around here." Anna sighed contently in her husband's arms. "Did you ever think that this valley would be so busy?"

"I have Nate to thank for that," Ethan grumbled, but there was a twinkle in his eyes. "He started it when he brought all you women here last year. My life turned upside down since then."

Anna laughed. "Admit it, you like it. Cora saw through you from the start. It took me a while longer, but I quickly realized that your grumpy exterior was just an act. Underneath it all, you're just a big, loveable bear."

Ethan hugged her close. "It took the right woman to make me shed that outer layer, but that doesn't mean I have to admit that to my brothers." He kissed her slowly, his mouth lingering on hers.

"Cora sure was glad to have you back, and she didn't waste any time to tell me 'I told you so.'"

"About what?"

Ethan grinned. "That it suited me better if I smiled more."

Anna wrapped her arms around his neck and combed her fingers through his hair. "It's hard to believe that Caroline is leaving next spring to go to college."

Ethan stared down at her, a wide smile on his face. "That explains why Trevor was looking so sullen at supper."

Anna nodded. "He doesn't want her to leave. I'm surprised you noticed."

Ethan rolled to his back, bringing Anna on top of him. "There are a lot of things I notice, Anna Wilder. More than you will ever know."

Anna sighed. "Things will be different with her gone, but there will be other changes, too. To think there's going to be a baby born here in the valley in a few months."

"Cora's beside herself happy that you'll be here for the birth, and Harley will be happy like a buck in spring when he has a grandbaby to bounce on his lap."

"Maybe someday soon, we'll have one of our own." Heat crept up into Anna's cheeks at the intense shimmer of love in her husband's eyes.

He kissed her again and murmured, "You'll make a wonderful mother. I watched how good you were with that little girl."

"And I know you'll make a great father."

Ethan's hold on her tightened. His arms trembled. "I've realized how important family is to me, and thanks to you, I don't push them away any longer."

He gazed up into her eyes, his face suddenly serious. "I'm still sorry I was too late to salvage the wagon with all your belongings and things from home."

Anna leaned in closer. "Things can be replaced, but my home is here, with you. And," she smiled, touching her lips to his, "I'm eager to start making new memories with you."

Also by Peggy L Henderson

<u>Yellowstone Romance Series:</u>
(in recommended reading order)

Yellowstone Heart Song
Return to Yellowstone (novella)
A Yellowstone Christmas (novella)
Yellowstone Homecoming (novella)
Yellowstone Redemption
A Yellowstone Season of Giving (short story)
Yellowstone Awakening
Yellowstone Dawn
Yellowstone Deception
A Yellowstone Promise (novella)
Yellowstone Origins
Yellowstone Legacy

<u>Teton Romance Trilogy</u>

Teton Sunrise
Teton Splendor
Teton Sunset
Teton Season of Joy

<u>Second Chances Time Travel Romance Series</u>

Come Home to Me
Ain't No Angel
Diamond in the Dust

Blemished Brides

In His Eyes
In His Touch
In His Arms

Wilderness Brides

Cora's Pride
Anna's Heart

About the Author

Peggy L Henderson is an award-wining, best-selling western historical and time travel romance author of the Yellowstone Romance Series, Second Chances Time Travel Romance Series, Teton Romance Trilogy, and the Blemished Brides Western Historical Romance Series. She was also a contributing author in the unprecedented 50-book American Mail Order Brides Series, contributing Book #15, Emma: Bride of Kentucky.

When she's not writing about Yellowstone, the Tetons, or the old west, she's out hiking the trails, spending time with her family and pets, or catching up on much-needed sleep. She is happily married to her high school sweetheart. Along with her husband and two sons, she makes her home in Southern California.

I am always happy to hear from my readers! You can reach me via email at ynpdreamer@gmail.com

Website: peggylhenderson.com